ORI-
THE LOST
VERNDARI

ORIANA STAR

For information contact;
www.orianastar.com

Cover design by StoneVoodoo

ISBN: 978-1-7360394-1-0

First Edition: December 2020

To all those that stay by my side as I chase all my crazy dreams.

TABLE OF CONTENTS

PROLOGUE: **18 YEARS EARLIER** 8

1: **ORI** 14

2: **MASTER KAI** 21

3: **RYUU** 26

4: **ORI** 31

5: **DAIN** 35

6: **CEDRICK** 40

7: **ORI** 46

8: **CEDRICK** 50

9: **ORI** 54

10: **CEDRICK** 58

11: **ORION** 63

12: **MASTER KAI** 68

13: **CEDRICK** 72

14: **ORI** 76

15: **KHALID** 79

16: **ORI** 85

17: **ORI** 90

18: **CEDRICK** 97

19 **ORI:** 101

20: **MASTER KAI** 106

21: **ORI** 111

22: **CEDRICK** 117

23: **RYUU** 122

24: **ORI** 126

25: **UNKNOWN** 133

26: **ORI** 136

27: **BARRETT** 140

28: **KHALID** 145

29: **ORI** 150

30: **ORI** 156

31: **GYLFI** 163

32: **ORI** 171

33: **UNKNOWN** 175

34: **ORI** 179

35: **ORION** 184

36: **ORI.** 188

37: **UNKNOWN** 191

38: **RYUU** 195

39: **HEADMASTER** 200

40: **CEDRICK** 207

41: **ORI** 212

42: **RYUU** 218

43: **ORI** 223

44: **ORI** 228

45: **ORI** 232

46: **ORI** 237

47: **RYUU** 247

48: **ORI** 251

49: **BARRETT** 258

50: **UNKNOWN** 263

51: **ORI** 269

52: **ORI** 273

EPILOGUE: **THE MISTRESS** 277

Trigger Warning

This is a Fantasy Reverse Harem Romance with MPOV intended for readers 18+. Some topics contained in this book touch on sensitive issues that may be difficult for some readers. Contains scenes with explicit sexual content, crude language, violence, physical and sexual abuse. If this content offends and/or is a trigger, please DO NOT read this book.

A Note from the Author

Thanks for taking a chance and reading my debut novel. This book is largely self-edited. If you find an error that I've missed, please feel free to contact me directly, Orianastarwriting@gmail.com. I am happy to fix mistakes that I've missed, and I appreciate the help.

Thank You and Happy Reading!

-Oriana

PROLOGUE: 18 YEARS EARLIER

Power belongs to those who crave it the least

-Ljot

As the sun rises, the beauty of the day ahead is lost on me. I have been staring out the window, watching as time passes me by. Every second I dream of a life where I can hide from the reality that stalks me. I've seen it hiding in the shadows for the last nine months, waiting for its moment to strike. A strike that will come regardless of how much I allow myself to live in denial.

The pinks and purples that paint the morning sky do nothing to cover my pain. They do nothing to slow the inevitable. They cannot stop time. Where I would normally see beauty, I see only my pain. The rise of the sun is the beginning of my end. The day ahead will be my torment.

Standing at the hospital room window, my precious baby, Ori, lies in my arms. The machines in the room are only monitoring me, ensuring very few hospital personnel know about her. She was born with a mix of silver and red hair that is fascinating. Her charcoal gray eyes sparkle slightly every time the light hits them. I would give anything for the chance to raise her and watch her grow. I want to see her take her first steps, speak her first words, teach her right from wrong, while teaching her about our world. That chance was stolen from me the moment I found out I was giving birth to a girl. Her bastard of a father is power hungry and will destroy all that is unique about her in his search for power. She would never survive childhood if I were to keep her. Her father's anger and rage forced my hand. Protecting her is imperative, so I will do what any good mother in my situation would do. I'm sending her away to live with the humans. Our kind will never consider looking for her there. It will give her time to grow up away from our culture. She needs to learn to be strong for she will need that strength when she inevitably comes back into our society.

Looking down at my daughter for what is my last time, I hear, "It's time" from the nurse behind me. The nurse's silent steps gave me no clues to the limited time I have with my daughter. My only warning was the sound of the metal rings of the curtain sliding open. I will never be ready to give her up, but it is my only option.

No one in Verndari Society would condone my actions; I can't trust any of them. So, I turned to my human nurse for help. She has been helping me plan my daughter's escape since the moment I found out I was having a girl. Being human, I could trust her over any Verndari. We are going to make everyone think my daughter is dead. It's the only way to ensure my daughter is safe for the first eighteen years of her life. After that Ori is on her own.

"Just a few more moments," I say, trying not to beg as silent tears fall down my cheeks onto the pale blue hospital gown I'm still wearing. I would happily beg if I thought it would help. But I know better. I know the answer before I hear it. My tears flow freely as the nurse confirms my worst fear.

"There is no time. We must get your daughter out before he arrives. You know this. If we fail, all the planning will be for naught." Her voice held no anger, just understanding. She states the facts with a gentle sternness that only those in her profession can manage.

I cradle my daughter close to my chest and give her one last kiss on her forehead. My eyes instinctually close as I whisper the words, "I will always love you" into her ear hoping to cement it into her being. The nurse slowly approaches me and takes my daughter. I watch the nurse as she carries my daughter out of the white hospital room, we have called home for the past 6 hours. Knowing this was happening doesn't make reality any easier. My entire body shakes: when I can no longer see them, I collapse onto the white tile floor feeling my heart break. The only remaining sounds are the beeping of my heart monitor.

Thundering footsteps sound from down the hall, breaking through the relative silence. You can hear the pounding of each step on the sterile tile hospital floor. His anger evident with every step he takes. I am not surprised when he storms into the room. At almost seven feet tall, the man towers over everyone. His silver hair lets everyone know just how powerful he is. That, combined with his size, is intimidating. Adding the scowl that is always present on his face, people run in the opposite direction.

I school my face, hiding my relief that I got my baby girl out in time. On the outside, I am crying at my loss. On the inside, I am jumping with joy that she is safe. It's impossible to know what kind of life she will have. But my girl will be alive; he will never find out about her.

"Where is she?" he booms, staring at me with eyes of steel. He suspects something is up; I see it in his eyes every time he looks at me. I have denied all accusations and I plan on keeping it that way. Not knowing how to answer, I let my tears continue to fall down my cheeks. My obvious distress is the only answer he will receive.

"The baby was stillborn, sir." The nurse says from behind him. "Give her some time. Losing a child is hard on any mother." His head quickly snaps in the nurse's direction and he glares at her for interrupting him. My husband has always thought he was above everyone else. His mannerisms instill the fear necessary to ensure people don't do stupid shit... like interrupt him. Personally, I enjoy watching the scene unfold.

"Who the hell are you?" He growls at her.

"I am your wife's nurse. I was there as she gave birth to your stillborn daughter. She is devastated, and rightfully so. Your attitude is not helping her heal after her lose." She says with such empathy it's impossible to tell the truth from the lies.

"My wife knows it was her only job to give birth to my daughter. My daughter being dead is no one's fault but hers." He sneers as he approaches her, getting within an inch of her face.

My nurse looks up at him, never wavering from her loyalty to me. "Your wife has just been through hell."

"The sole reason I am allowing you to still breathe is because we are in a hospital. Even I can't get away with killing you here. But I will come after you. No one speaks to me like you have and gets away with it. Enjoy watching over your shoulder for the rest of your life." My husband threatens.

I will be eternally grateful to my nurse for everything that she had done for me and my baby girl. She is putting herself at risk by helping us. She is risking her life lying to the man in front of me. But to her it was worth the risk; I can see it in her eyes. She is a beautiful soul that has been my confidant these past nine months and knows everything that I have gone through. She told me multiple times that she would willingly risk her life for an innocent child, especially if it means keeping my child away from him. She may be human, but I've taught her what being a female Verndari means. She understands there are more risks than just the physical abuse my child would inevitably experience. We need to keep my child's power from him. He is already dangerous; he does not need the power my daughter would give him.

I watch as he catalogues her one last time. My nurse never flinches under his assessing eyes. She glances at me one last time. When I give her a nod, she turns and leaves me alone with the man from my nightmares. Once he is certain she is nowhere in sight, he looks back at me; "If I find out you're lying to me... you're dead." he promises as he struts out the door caring about only himself. Why was my daughter doomed to have him as a father?

1: ORI

Being a Verndari Female is an Honor.... But sometimes it sucks!

-Ljot

One more day I repeat to myself over and over again in an effort to stop myself from breaking. Lying face down on the hardwood of my foster father's desk is a familiar experience. This time, he has my shirt lifted to my shoulders and is burning cigars onto my back. Every burn causes his office to fill with the smell of my burning flesh. My teeth clench as I stop myself from screaming. I will never let him hear me scream.

I count the burns to eleven before his heavy footsteps pound on the hardwood floor, signifying the end of this session. I stay still until I hear his office door slam shut behind me. At his departure, I finally release the breath I was holding. Standing up, I wince as my shirt falls down my back. His office is dark with no windows. He likes it that way; nobody can see what happens in here. His carpet has burn marks scattered around where he has let his cigars fall to the ground. I'm surprised he hasn't burnt the house down. All four office walls have holes that expose the electrical wires and plumbing. A characteristic he has found useful on more than one occasion. The solid wood door separating his office from the hallway is the only unbroken part of the room.

I quickly slip out of the room, making sure to quietly close the door behind me. If he hears me leave, he will come back for more. I sneak through the hallway and up the stairs before I make it back to my room. This room doesn't look like much, but it is mine.

I walk over to the burgundy curtains and score the last mark onto the wall. The burgundy curtains are too big for the window in my room and hide the marks. I hated those curtains at first, but grew to love their awkwardness, especially once I started my get out of jail countdown. I smile, knowing my escape from this life is only hours away. Scoring the wall each night has been my countdown to leaving this hellhole. I made the first score on my sixteenth birthday. I remember that day like it was yesterday. It was the day my life changed forever. My life as a foster child was never rainbows, but it definitely wasn't the hell that I endured from that point forward.

I lived in this home for a month before that night. The home had 3 other foster children. They ranged in ages from twelve to seventeen years old. None of them talked; silence was their constant companion. The few times we interacted; fear was palpable in their eyes. It was like they were always waiting for the shoe to drop. My time bouncing around homes taught me to trust the looks in people's eye's - looks of fear, sadness, grief, happiness, depression, anxiety, trauma. They all tell me about my environment, helping me to survive. The looks in the three children's eyes told me this home was the worst they had ever been placed in. I just didn't know why.

That all changed on my 16th birthday. Did I wish to stay naïve to the horrors of this home? Definitely. Who wouldn't? Do I regret my actions that day? I wouldn't have changed a thing.

Like any other day, we were gathered quietly around the dinner table. The food they gave us was minimal, but I was never stupid enough to question it. I was almost done eating, rushing through the food, aiming for a fast escape, when "father" walked in. His face full of anger and rage. I watched as he dragged the youngest of us, Noelani, aside. Before I even realized what was happening, he had her tied up and began whipping her. Her scream will be forever engrained in my mind. I knew I couldn't allow it to continue.

It didn't matter what set him off. I shot out of my seat, stepping in the way, protecting her from the beating. I clenched my teeth with each hit of the whip but refused to show him any weakness. Noelani screamed in my ear every time the whip cracked. I don't know how long it lasted. I stayed in front of her until "father" left, slamming the front door behind him. She got out shortly after that; for which I am grateful. Any home is better than this hell.

After that day, I became their favorite, receiving all their attention. Attention that I didn't want. Unfortunately for me, the kids that had been in the home the longest became jealous. They have grown to need the brutal attention. Pain became a new daily occurrence. If the fosters weren't dueling it out, the other kids were. The others had long since been brain washed. That is when I finally understood just how alone I was. I started my countdown to freedom that night. So far, I have scored 703 days into my wall. I chuckled to myself, glad that I won't be here when the fosters find it. I can only imagine the reaction they will have.

The burgundy curtains clash with the lime green and black bedding that covers my "bed". Technically, it's a bed, but it is so dilapidated that I'm sure some people would disagree with its bed status. Who am I trying to kid, it shouldn't even be called a bed. It's stained and worn with age. With no box-spring, the mattress sits on the floor. The sheet that covers it only slightly hides the many rips and tears that are present. Through the years I have figured out the perfect places to sleep on that pathetic thing, but recently I have been woken up to springs poking me in the back. Not the best sensation.

My backpack, used and abused through the years, is mine and sits on my bed. Even though I found it used, I made it work. Now, it's held together with more duct tape than fabric. Some people call it trash, but I like to call it unique.

Everything important from my life is in this backpack, my journals that would get me committed if someone read them, my boots, the only thing I have ever bought, and any money I successfully hid. A couple grand sits hidden at the bottom of my pack. That money would be taken from me in a heartbeat if they knew I had it. Thankfully, I'm great at hiding things. I grab my bag and carefully drop it out the window into the bushes below. It's imperative that I get it out of the house before the fosters kick me out, a fact that I am not sad about.

I stay by the window quietly listening for the thud indicating that my bag has reached its ultimate destination. When I hear it safely land, I allow my exhaustion to take over and I collapse on my "bed".

A loud knock at the door wakes me. "Fuck I should have left by now." I mumble as my foster mother screams about coming into the room. Her voice has always made me cringe. It's one of those high-pitched screechy voices that are about as nice as nails on a chalkboard. To be honest, her appearance isn't much better. Sitting on the shorter side at barely 5 ft tall, her greasy blond hair is always unkempt, and she has a disheveled look about her. Her teeth are stained from the coffee that seems permanently glued to her hand. Honestly, it took some genuine effort to learn how to look at her without cringing.

"What the HELL are you still doing here? I told you I wanted you out before the sun rose. Get out of my house, Ori!" She demands as her voice gets higher and more screechy with every word she speaks.

"I'm leaving." I say with a huff as I fumble out of bed. I'll be glad to never see this house again. She may want me gone, but I'm positive that my desire to leave and never look back is greater.

I glance out my window for the last time as I see the sun is rising above the horizon. Today's sunrise is just as beautiful as all the others I have watched. It's filled with beautiful pinks and oranges. Sunrise is my favorite time of day; the view from my window was the only enjoyable thing I had in this house. No one here understands my fascination with the sunrise. I don't always understand it myself, but my need to appreciate its beauty is deeply engrained; I can't stop myself from trying to imprint this view into my head.

I say my usual morning thank-yous to mother nature when I suddenly get a blinding pain in my head. I can't stop the scream that escapes me; it is the first time I have allowed myself to scream since coming here. The pain in my head is intense and I feel like my head will explode. My foster father's abuse is nothing compared to the pain I am now feeling. My control has finally slipped; I can no longer control my reactions as my hands go to my head of their own accord and my body collapses. My head hits the hard floor and my vision blurs as I watch my foster mother walking towards me. Behind her, my foster father and the other kids all enter, circling around me. With each step closer they take, my pain increases, before my vision finally gives out. "Fuck" I scream as darkness finally consumes me.

2: MASTER KAI

The Awakening is both memorable and painful.

-Ljot

I've been teaching at this academy for the past 60 years. Every member of our kind grace these halls at one point or another. The class I am teaching is advanced magic and has twenty young men. These men are the twenty brightest at our school. They have a larger amount of power and the ability to perform advanced magic.

Two of my best students are Orion and Barrett. They are a year apart in age and are one of a handful of individuals whose power is expressed in their physical appearance. Orion absorbs information like a sponge, always craving more. The more he learns and the more control he gains, the brighter his blue hair becomes; his magic craves the knowledge as much as his mind does. Barrett's magic is so naturally powerful that it has hindered his physical growth. He is by far the shortest Verndari I have ever seen and has been bald since birth. A unique characteristic of his that he has learned to love through the years.

Today we are testing on the many ways that mental magic can be used. The test has both a written portion and a physical test. Half the class is sitting in desks writing frantically, hoping to complete the written part of the exam in time. The other half I've paired up; they're testing in the back of the room, demonstrating their skills.

"How much time do we have left Master Kai?" Orion asks from the front of the room.

"10 Minutes before we switch." I answer. Loud groans from the students tell me some might not finish. That is a shame.

In the back I watch the minds of the students to see how successful they are at implanting a full memory. Some students mastered this technique right away, some students are still struggling. The blast hit when the second set of students was implanting memories.

To say the blast was a shock is an understatement. It came at us like a freight train. I felt the power of the Awakening hit my system and it was so strong that my knees gave out, causing me to collapse onto the desk next to me. I honestly don't remember the last time an Awakening affected me... a century at least. I can only imagine the power this gentleman will hold.

A lot... significantly more than anyone else in this room. When I look around my classroom, all 20 of the students have collapsed. The lucky ones are leaning on one of my many bookshelves. Some have fully collapsed on the ground with their tests and supplies now scattered about. Some students are screaming, while others are just moaning, no one is immune.

I close my eyes and hunt for the source of the Awakening; a rare gift which has come in handy once or twice. This occurrence doesn't differ from my past experiences. I follow the remnants of the surge to the origin point. The remnants are a road of glitter that was left behind, making it easy to follow. Everyone's remnants are different, with varying shades of colors and sparkles that cross the spectrum from barely noticeable to blinding. The remnants in question are a mix of pinks and teals with a sparkle that reminds me of the stars in the night sky. It only takes a few minutes for me to reach the origin point. The moment I do, I swear in a manner that would make my mother frown.

"Fuck" I shout as I run straight for the Headmaster. No longer caring about the students in pain. They will live. There are more important things. I hear the doors to my classroom slam shut behind me as I race through the halls.

The halls of the school, only lit up by wall sconces, are still fairly dark since the sun hasn't risen high enough yet for the daylight to brighten our halls. The darkness doesn't bother me; I have walked these halls long enough that I could walk them blind if need be.

The Headmaster's office is on the other side of the school, so even running, I take about three minutes to make it to the two large wooden double doors. Knocking is usually vital, but fuck formalities. I throw the doors open, and as soon as I enter, I hear the deep rumbling of the Headmaster; frustration that we rarely hear is clear in his tone.

"Where is our fresh addition and how did we not know someone was coming of age?" The Headmaster practically screams as I enter his office. The Headmaster is still fairly young for being in his position. At 300 years old, he looks to be in his thirties to mortals. His dark black hair is disheveled, and his clothes have a thrown-on appearance. I get the suspicion that even he was affected by the Awakening. Normally he is a very welcoming man, but in times of stress he can be scary; you don't want to end up on the Headmaster's bad side.

"With the humans." I answer quickly, knowing just how imperative it is that we get to the individual quickly. "About 400 miles from here. You need to call Ryuu's team."

"You know I'm not supposed to do that." The Headmaster says. "Who else?"

"No one else is close enough. They are four miles away. We need someone there now." I say with urgency. We both know the devastating effect an Awakening has on both the individual and society around them. There is no guessing the outcome, all Awakenings are different. The powers in the individual are jump started. What their powers are determines if the public is safe or not; regardless, the awakening always hurts the person going through it.

A controlled Awakening ensured a safe location, protecting him and those around them. We'd have someone on medical on standby to help ease the pain and ensuring the transition is smoother. Only a handful of people who have gone through their Awakening without the proper medical support. One such individual is on Ryuu's team. Another reason they are the best option. Not only are they closest, they have someone that will truly understand what our recent addition is going through.

The Headmaster sighs before finally giving in and quickly picking up the phone. While I don't envy the upcoming conversation, I'm glad I don't have to spend 10 minutes arguing with the Headmaster; that is time we don't have. Time is not on our side. It is imperative that we get to the origin quickly.

Unfortunately, knowing that calling in Ryuu's team is the right thing to do, doesn't stop me from mentally cringing. It will not be pretty. Ryuu's team is supposed to be on a break. A much-needed break. If their vacation ended in a few days, I wouldn't be so worried, but their time off just started… four hours ago. He will be pissed.

3: RYUU

Embrace the Quiet Times

-Ljot

W e arrive late at night. Darkness had long since covered the sky and the bright moon was high, helping to guide our way home. The place we call home is in the country, on the outskirts of Tarengill. It is deep in the woods, allowing us much-needed privacy. The stars are sparkling in the sky; a beautiful scene that brings all four of us peace when we need it most. Coming upon our drive took weight off my shoulders; I feared they would cancel our vacation before it even started.

After being gone for three straight months on Council orders, we negotiated this much-needed vacation. This is our first real vacation in about ten years. Vacations are a luxury that individuals in our positions just aren't given; we all plan on taking full advantage of the time we are given. Who knows when the Council will give us another opportunity.

For the past three months, the four of us have been living off minimal sleep: most nights only receiving three hours of sleep each night. Our bodies have long since been functioning off adrenaline alone. As soon as my foot finally stepped over the threshold of our house, my body understood that it could finally shut down. I was sleepwalking up the stairs to my room and crashing on my bed before I even took my shoes off. I remember looking forward to a day of sleeping in. Something so simple, yet unattainable.

I was in a nice deep sleep when the blinding pain of an Awakening woke us all up; an unpleasant way to start your day.

"Why the fuck didn't they warn us." Dain grumbles from next to me. Dain is the smallest of the group at 5 ft 9. His bald head is doing nothing for his height, but he is the best of us. His compassion and understanding know no bounds. He won't be mad for long. Give it five minutes.

"Good fucking question." I reply. I'm pissed and unlike Dain, I will be furious for some time. My phone ringing only seconds later just adds to my increasing frustrations. The Council knows that we are to be left alone; I thought I had gotten that fact through their thick skulls. Fumbling around with my phone, it takes me three rings to see that the Headmaster of the academy is calling. The Headmaster was the councilman who helped to push our vacation through; he is the last person I expected to be calling. My thoughts go a million directions, but the only conclusion I came to is that whatever happened had to be bad. He would only call if it was an absolute emergency. That doesn't stop me from expressing my frustrations.

"Why didn't you warn us of the Awakening?" I ask before he can get any words in. I'm agitated and pissed off. Everything changes when he informs me that nobody knew that the Awakening was going to happen.

"What do you mean no one knew? We always know." That caused Dain to sit up in a blink of an eye. I can feel him lean in closer trying to hear what is being said, nosy little shit.

I listen in stunned silence as he tells me what little they know. I am not surprised to hear that Kai worked his magic to find the location of the Awakening; I wouldn't have expected anything less. Without his gift, finding our new Verndari would have been impossible. Finding out that the new Verndari is in the human sector has me gasping in shock. It has been about 75 years since someone awakened around humans. I wasn't part of the team that retrieved him, but the scene that unfolded is legendary and is studied at the academy by everyone. The destruction and devastation that occurred in the ten minutes it took to get to him took years to fix. There is a heavyweight on his conscious over what transpired. He had no control, which he understands, but it doesn't stop him from holding himself responsible.

I am not surprised when the Headmaster asks us to be the retrieval team, but I still must advocate for my men. We deserve time off. "Can't someone else do it?" I ask him after hearing his request. "We just got back". I know the question was futile, but I had to ask. If not for me, for my guys.

They spread teams like ours out all around the world so it is no surprise to hear we are the closest by at least 50 miles; he wouldn't have called us if there was someone closer. No matter how much the four of us want a vacation, we aren't going to stand by and let one of our own suffer.

"Send Dain the coordinates." I demand, immediately flipping to work mode. I glance over at Dain. Seconds later, he nods, indicating we have received the coordinates. "You can count on us Headmaster." I say as I begin quickly getting dressed.

The centuries spent being the Council's lackey has created a switch in my brain. As soon as I flick it on, nothing else but the job matters. The sleep my body so desperately craved not hours earlier is now an afterthought; our mission is all that matters now.

By the time I hang up, my entire team is in my room. All three men are ready to go. "Where to boss?" Cedrick asks, not even questioning why our vacation got cut short. Cedrick is the most laid-back of our group. At 6 ft 8 inches he has the hardest time blending in, but I can always depend on him to be there. Especially for this. Honestly, if I turned down the job, he probably wouldn't forgive me. Who am I kidding, there is no probably about it; we would have lost him if I turned it down. He told me once that the retrievals we complete help him redeem himself after what happened during his Awakening. It's why I rarely turn them down. This retrieval, though, is more significant.

"An unknown individual just had there Awakening. No one knows who they are, so we are going in blind. We are to go retrieve them and safely transport them to the institute."

"Why us?" Dain asked next to me. "They rarely send us on retrievals." He is right. They typically save us for the recon missions or their dirty work.

"The individual is four miles from us and in the human settlement."

"Fuck!" Cedrick grunts as he starts and bolts out the door, not even waiting for my next commands. I expected nothing less from him, as he is the only one out of all of us who truly understands what it means to awaken around humans.

He doesn't talk about that time in his life. All we know is what they have taught at the institution. Only Cedrick knows what he truly went through that day, but we can all see the pain on his face whenever the topic is broached. If his reaction to our new mission is any indication, I'd say I wouldn't have been able to keep him from going. This is personal for him.

4: ORI

Pain, the Beginning of a New Life

-Ljot

I don't know how long I was passed out. In the past, when I blacked out, my body ached, but the initial pain would have already subsided. The intensity of the aches always let me know how long I was out. Upon waking up, my pounding head indicated that I wasn't out long. The pain is so intense, I can feel my heartbeat through my head. I feel worse now than before I blacked out. A definite first for me. This felt different.

My foster "mother" was screaming at me to get out of her house. This intensified the pain I was in. I am used to her yelling. But something was different this time. Usually when she yells, I just roll my eyes at her because once again she is being ridiculous; it was a frequent occurrence in this house.

This time though, when she screams at me, I feel her hatred of me like it was my own. The intensity behind it is shocking and painful. I knew she didn't like me, but the reality of her feelings is far worse than I could have ever imagined. Why does she hate me so much? The emotions I was feeling were so intense that it drowned out the others entering the room. It is only when I felt emotions coming at me from all angles that I realize the others must have joined her. The combination of my "mother's" hatred, my "father's" sickening fascination, and my foster sibling's jealousy, drowned out my own emotions. I could no longer feel my own emotions. It felt as if their feelings were mine. Even though my head knew differently, I still couldn't find my way through their feelings to reach my own. I was spiraling and wanted all the foreign feelings to disappear. Why won't they go away?

At some point my hands clung to my head, trying to find relief. Little drops of blood dripping down the side of my head clued me into the fact that my nails were digging into my skin. This unintentional self-mutilation was the least of my priorities. When I can finally take a moment to open my eyes, I find myself surrounded. It shocked me. Even though the emotions I was feeling told me they were all here, I still didn't want to believe it. Why can't I trust my gut?

My pain continues to intensify as their emotions gain strength. Under these circumstances, it doesn't take a genius to figure out that I needed to get away from everyone; being alone sounds like heaven. I suddenly pray for a solitude that would take away the unwanted emotions. Assuming I am correct, I get my ass in gear, and try to crawl my way out of the house. But it was no use. I barely made it a foot before the pressure built to the point where it felt like my head would explode. I had to move closer to them in order to get away. With every inch closer I made it, more pressure built in my head until it stopped me dead in my tracks. I screamed a never-ending scream that was so loud I'm sure the neighbors heard. How the hell am I going to extricate myself?

I didn't hear the footsteps, but soon I feel myself being lifted by gentle hands. It was a strange sensation that eased my pain slightly. Gentleness is foreign to me. I wish to wrap myself in the feeling and never let it go. Unfortunately for me, the negative thoughts overpowered the wonderful feelings of safety I had felt.

"We got you, sweetheart." Someone says to me in a soothing voice. The sound feeling like a gentle caress unlike anything I have ever felt before. I loved the second when the caress dulled my pain. Unfortunately for me, it felt ten times worse when the pain came back.

"Please, just kill me." I mumble, unable to take anymore. The longer I was feeling their emotions, the more negativity seemed to implant itself inside my head. I can't feel anything else. We've barely stepped foot outside of my room when suddenly images of me killing myself come into my head like they are the best ideas in the world. I can't stop the whimper that escapes me. After everything I've been through, I never thought about killing myself. Why would it happen now? It wouldn't. I know it wouldn't. These aren't feelings, images, or memories that are mine; they are someone else's deranged ideas. The problem is... my mind doesn't know the difference. FUCK!

"We've got to hurry." Someone else with a deep voice says urging the person carrying me forward. Yes... get me the fuck out of this hellhole. Any place is better than here. I think as another unwanted image enters my mind. FUCK! Make it stop! Please make it stop!

"Grab her stuff." Someone commands from behind me. Even this man's commanding voice seems to slightly sooth the pain. Could they just keep talking? Too bad I'm in no state to communicate.

From behind me I hear my "mother" sneer, "She doesn't have any stuff." I could feel the person holding me tense up. If he wasn't holding me, I'm sure he would have given her a piece of his mind. How do I know that? It's like I can sense his anger toward her. Join the club buddy, I think, as we get further and further away from my "family." When the time comes, he will have to get in line because I call dibs.

The creak of the bottom step breaks through my senses, forcing me to speak up. "Bushes... It's in the bushes." I mumble so softly that I'm not sure they heard me. I wish I could speak louder, but it is the best I can do. All I hope is that they heard me and can find my bag. My entire world is in that bag. My bag isn't much, but it is mine, I think, right before I pass out ... again. I really hope this doesn't become a habit. It makes me feel weak. I refuse to be weak.

5: DAIN

Never Forget the Power a Woman Holds

-Ljot

Quickly guiding everyone through the streets of Tarengill, we make it to a dilapidated part of town. Tarengill is one of the poorest human settlements around. The humans of Tarengill have been rejected by all alternative settlements. They are the outcasts of human society.

They should have torn down most of these houses ages ago. Every house we pass has chipped paint, holes in their roofs, boarded up shutters, or broken windows. Proper housing has been long forgotten in Tarengill.

The sun has almost fully risen as we make our way through town. A few humans are mingling outside and they all glare at us as we move through the streets. The looks don't surprise us. Most humans are weary of us; nobody blames them. These days, humans are the lowest in our society and typically get the least amount of resources. Their contempt for us is understandable. Unfortunately for them, their ancestor's unwillingness to accept the Verndari resulted in the world we have today.

When I finally stop us at an intersection, I turn and easily sense the newly awoken in the house at the very end of the street. The house is a two-story house, the mint green paint is chipping and has seen better days, the cement driveway is cracked and uneven, the shutters are barely hanging on, and the roof probably should have been replaced years ago. I'll be surprised if there are no holes in their roof.

As soon as I point out the house to the others, Cedrick bolts straight for it, slamming the door open. He takes 30 seconds max to get from our position at the opposite side of the street to the house in question; the rest of us are hot on his heels. Seconds after entering the home we all hear a woman scream. Thinking the worst, I prepare myself for the inevitable, protecting humans from one of our own.

What we end up finding, shocks us all. There are five humans standing in a circle screaming at someone. There are two older individuals, most likely the heads of the house, along with three children, two adolescent girls and a teenage boy. The children and adults alike are equally angry. The children in question are in ragged clothes that have seen better days. Their dirty skin and tangled hair make us wonder when the last time was that they took a shower.

Out of the two adults, the man alone had a clean appearance. He reminded me of a businessman in his clean-cut suit, shiny shoes, and hair in perfect condition; he looks out of place. His wife was in only slightly better condition than the kids. While you could at least tell she has showered, her make-up was caked on thick enough that her skin looked white. Her stained twisted teeth, white ratty hair, and stained clothes contrasted from her husband's perfect appearance. What the hell?

With no time for contemplation, I allow my instincts to take over; I pull the closest of the human's out of the way. The human I moved is the wife. She looks to be approximately fifty years old, and she carries a look of contempt on her face. It has been a long time since I've seen that much anger in one person. As I continue to pull her out of the way, Ryuu and Gylfi corral the others away, giving us a better view of the center of the circle.

What I didn't expect was the scene in front of us. In the center lays a woman clutching her head, screaming. Curled up in a ball, it's impossible to tell her height, but her hair is beautiful. The silver and blood red hair stands out against her pale skin. Upon closer examination, you can see drops of blood coating the ends of her hair.

I knew instantly that she was our newly awoken. I didn't have time to register what finding another female really meant. Getting her away from here is my number one priority. I gently scoop her up into my arms.

"We got you, sweetheart." I say carrying her away from the human's tormenting her. Cedrick, who was stuck in the doorway, has his fists clenched and quickly follows behind.

"Just kill me." She mumbles still clutching her head.

I immediately look over at Cedrick. The look of concern on his face tells me everything that I need to know. I quickly speed up and jog down the stairs. I briefly hear Ryuu tell Gylfi to grab her stuff. When the humans inform us that the girl in my arms owns nothing, I barely catch the mumbled "bushes" come out of her voice.

Cedrick must have heard; as soon as we exit the home, he immediately goes to the bushes around the side of the house. I trust him to hunt for the girl's things. I jog out of town, knowing he will be right behind us.

It only takes a few minutes for the others to catch up to me. Cedrick has a small, threadbare bookbag hanging from his shoulder. I'm not even sure you can call it a bookbag anymore. There are a few patches of the original black fabric, but she has patched together the rest of it with multiple colors of duct tape. There is mainly silver with red and black mixed in.

"Is that all there was?" I ask, not really wanting to know the answer.

"Yeah." He says with sadness that we haven't heard from him in a long time. I internally cringe knowing that this is wreaking havoc on his mind. A reminder of the darkest time of his life, I need not see into Cedrick's mind to understand the difficulty he is facing.

"She has been through more than I have." Cedrick suddenly says in a solemn voice, breaking me out of my thoughts. "Don't let go of her Dain. She needs the comfort your providing. It's anchoring her to reality. At least for now." He continues making us all wonder how bad this girl's life has been. It took months for Cedrick to heal from what happened to him.

She is in for a lengthy recovery if what Cedrick says is true. I look back down at the woman in my arms and promise do to everything in my power to ensure she recovers from this. Hopefully, it will be enough.

6: CEDRICK

Power is best held by those who desire it least

-Ljot

The trip to the school was quiet. I could feel the guy's eyes on me; knowing my past, it worried them. They are afraid this experience will pull me into my own dark memories. My memories are nothing compared to the images going through her mind. Fake memories are integrating themselves with her genuine ones. The scary part… her actual memories are barely better than the fake ones. Since the moment I entered that fucking awful home, her mind's horrors have been playing repeatedly on a loop. I wish I could take them all away and replace them with memories of the life she should have had. She didn't deserve to go through everything she did.

Since my Awakening, I always thought my experience was the worst outcome possible. My parents, deciding to strengthen me, dropped me off deep in human territory, knowing full well I could never make it out in time. I remember running and barely making it halfway back when the Awakening hit me. My entire body surged with power and I could feel it sparking. I remember bolts of power escaping me every minute or so. I wanted to see the damage my power was causing, but I was experiencing too much pain to do anything. It took the Council an hour to find me. An hour that caused more damage not only to me mentally but also destroyed vast sections of the human settlement; they had never seen an Awakening that caused such extensive damage. I didn't learn about the damage I caused until after the fact; homes and businesses all went up in flames because of the power that escaped me. It took months for me to learn how to cope with the guilt and work past it.

The girl in Dain's arms has had years of pain. What she is experiencing is the tip of the iceberg. How is this going to affect her? I pray that her strength will get her through everything she has experienced.

It took months for me to overcome the damage that was created in an hour of my life. This woman has experienced years of constant abuse and pain. How long will it take her to learn to live?

I said a silent thank you when we finally reached the cobblestone path that leads to the school; it gives my mind something else to focus on. The school itself was built 500 years ago. The main building looks like a castle. You can see its pillars from miles away. Besides the main house, there are 5 other buildings on the grounds that are used for teaching the various focuses.

The Headmaster's office sits on the first floor of the main building. We are sitting there along with three other Council members. One of the Council members is the Headmaster. While his expression is very neutral, I'm positive he is on our side. The Headmaster is honorable. The other two are a different story. One of them looks to be in his sixties which means he is probably 700 years old; I doubt he would admit to his age. He has been giving us the runaround since we have arrived. I suspect he couldn't care less about what happens to the girl. The Council woman that is present has been silent during the entire exchange. I suspect she thinks the girl in Dain's arms is weak; her assumptions couldn't be any further from the truth. The young Verndari woman is the strongest person I have ever met. She kept rising from the ashes when most people would have fallen.

I am looking over at Dain, while half listening to the eldest Council member tell us again that they won't be helping the girl, I see that Dain still has the young girl protectively in his arms. Good man. He understands the importance of what he is doing. It may not seem like much, but it is everything the woman needs; it is her only light in the darkness that had taken over her mind.

"We have to find her mates now." I demand, focusing back on the man arguing with us. I feel like a broken record, arguing my points for the fifth time tonight. The Council members don't seem to understand the urgency of the situation. I feel like shaking some sense into them. You would think the older Verndari wouldn't be so stupid. Unfortunately for us, the old shmucks are stuck in their ways.

"You know we can't do that until she is awake." The oldest Council member says again like I didn't hear him the first time. There are exceptions to every rule, including this one. Unfortunately, the Council doesn't want to make any exceptions. Fucking jerks.

"Has it not occurred to you that her brain is keeping her unconscious for a reason." I start. "It's her body's way of protecting her." I point out, unable to keep my voice from rising.

"Protecting her from what?" The Headmaster asks. Unlike the others present, he seems genuinely curious. I've always liked that about him. The man seems to absorb knowledge like a sponge and can't resist asking questions when he doesn't know something.

"If she wakes up, she will kill herself." I state matter-of-factly causing everyone in the room to gasp, including the men I call my brothers. "It's all she's thinking about."

"How could you possibly know that?" I'm asked by the last Council member who is clearly pissed off. He would know if he ever paid any attention to the men they employ. My position is apparently so low to them they feel it's above them to know what their own men are capable of.

I snap at that moment, unable to hold anything back any longer. "I've spent the last two hours watching her kill herself repeatedly in her head. The emotions and desires of the humans got buried too deep. They now feel like her own. The only individuals who have a chance at helping her are her mates. You guys are aware of that."

"Just call everyone in for the ceremony. We'll try to get her conscious, but you need to be ready to start the ceremony immediately." Ryuu commands like it is us he is bossing around, not the Council. I am proud to be part of his team in that moment. Very few Verndari have the guts to speak to Council members like he just did; people are too afraid of the consequences.

"I already did." The Headmaster says stunning his two associates into silence. The looks they are giving him tell me they did not agree to the action. Lucky for us, they say nothing in our presence; the Council doesn't want to make a scene. But the looks they are sending the Headmaster's way would kill lesser men. I'm sure he has a lot of explaining to do.

"The last person just arrived." He continued as if he didn't notice the daggers his colleagues were sending him. "We will head to the hall and meet you there." He finishes and quickly ushers the other Council members out of the room.

My jaw would be on the floor if it wasn't connected to my face. The four of us remain silent as we watch them leave; too afraid they will change their mind. When the doors slam shut behind them, Dain breaks the silence by asking the question on all our minds.

"So… how are we going to wake her up?"

"Good fucking question."

7: ORI

Pain Brings New Life

-Ljot

I hear a deep voice calling to me, but I can barely hear it through the pain. I try to get closer to the voice, but the pain becomes more intense. I don't want to feel this pain any longer. I'm slipping back into the abyss. His voice is blocking my way, ensuring I stay with him. I feel the pain, but I also feel soothed by the sound of his voice.

"I know it hurts, but I need you to be strong and wake-up for a few minutes. It's important, sweetheart." The voice says coaxing me back to reality.

I feel myself coming back to consciousness, which is a double-edged sword. I am glad I'm awake; it means I'm not weak. I don't like feeling weak, but no matter how strong I believe myself to be, I still wish I'd just disappear. The pain is always present when I'm awake; blackness was so peaceful. Everything feels so much better there. When the darkness creeps in, two rough hands gently grab my cheeks.

"I know it feels better there, but we need you to be awake for us to help you." His deep soothing voice says. "Don't focus on the pain, just focus on my voice. Open your eyes, darling." He commands in such a gentle, but strong voice that I instinctually listen. His voice sooths a part of my soul that has felt abandoned. How could I not listen? He sounds like he actually cares what happens to me.

It takes a moment, but soon I'm prying my eyes open. The bright light that suddenly invades my vision is a shock to my system; I can't stop the whimper that escapes. "Good Girl." The man in front of me says with a smile that doesn't quite reach his beautiful chocolate brown eyes. His hair is so blond it looks as white as snow. It is beautiful; I wonder what it looks like under the sun? The thought briefly distracts me until a new image hits my head, causing me to whimper. Each new image that comes at me brings more fire and ache to my already aching head.

Even though I know they aren't real, it always feels like I'm there. This time I am in my old, dilapidated room and my foster brother is there. I watch him as he stalks closer to me. "You know you want to." He says in a sinister tone that I am way too familiar with. I try to say no, but nothing comes out of my mouth. It's like someone has stolen my voice. Instead of fighting, I watch in horror as I grab the knife handed to me. In a matter of seconds, I turn the knife on myself; I gasp and scream as I feel the knife go straight into my stomach. I can feel the pain as if it were all real. Blood flows like a river from the wound I created, when suddenly I hear that voice again.

"Come back to me." The soothing voice is saying somewhere in the background. "Come back." He says more forcefully, starting to sound more like a command. I'd love to, I think as I slip back to reality.

"I don't want to be here." I tell him between whimpers. I'd rather be in the black abyss where nothing exists, especially the pain. My mind won't be able to take much more.

"We can't help you if you disappear. Your mates can help you and we will find them, but we need you awake." He says in his soothing voice that I am cherishing. "Just focus on my beautiful chocolate brown eyes." He says with a smirk.

I'm still trying to register what he said when we start moving. The man holding me is trying to keep me still; a gentle sway, one of the few indicators of our movement. The man in front of me walks backwards; he keeps his eyes on mine with his hands holding my cheeks the entire trip. He is forcing me to stay focused on him and not our surroundings. I still see images flashing in the back of my mind, but they seem muted, like they are in a fog. He makes everything a little better; to which I am eternally grateful.

"Good girl." He says again as we walk through a set of double doors. Suddenly the Surrounding noise amplifies. I look away from the beautiful chocolate eyes to find hundreds of individuals gathered. The room I am in is huge, expensive, and crowded. I notice little else cause my mind slips again. Fuck! I shouldn't have looked away; without those calming eyes, I quickly slip into another nightmare.

This time I'm in my bedroom, standing in the middle of the closet. I'm alone this time, but I find a noose hung up in the closet and wrapped around my neck. When I look down, I discover that I am standing on a crate. A second later I feel myself falling as if the crate just disappeared from under me. The rope quickly tightens around my neck. My nails immediately start clawing at my throat, trying to make it so I can breathe. Nothing works… my eyes swiftly get spotty and darkness closes in. The closer I get to darkness, the more freedom I feel.

"Open your eyes and look at me." He says practically screaming. The feel of his hands on my cheeks combined with his always encouraging voice is something I can't say no to. I don't think I'll ever be able to say no. The guy I'm looking at has my head focused right on him. The depth of his eyes allows my bedroom and nightmare to disappear into a faint whisper just visible in the background.

"That's it. Just focus on me. Not much longer now." He says with a confidence that I can't help but cling to. "You will be just fine," he says.

I hope he is right because I can't live like this much longer.

8: CEDRICK

Mates are the Best Medicine

-Ljot

They better make this real fucking quick, I think, as I'm trying to pull her back to reality ... Again.

We had just entered the assembly area when something distracted her. In reality, I should have expected it. The assembly area is massive and filled with thousands of males. Shouts resonate all around in a strange mix of excitement and anger. The crowd itself doesn't hide the extravagance of this place, with statues made from gems and a glass ceiling that shows the beauty of the sky. Its lavishness is nothing like what she is used to.

I don't know what exactly triggered it, but as soon as she lost eye contact, she slipped under again. Every time she loses her grip on reality, it is getting harder and harder to reach her. Her mind is getting buried deep in the suggested memories that are being forced on her. My usual coaxing is no longer working; I had to scream to break through. She is getting worse.

"You need to make it quick," I shout over my shoulder as the young woman blinks and tries to refocus on me. "Good girl." I say again for what feels like the hundredth time. This time, I take her head in my hands, forcing her to stay focused on me. She doesn't fight me on it, which I am grateful for. Keeping her grounded is the only we have of keeping her in the present. If she slips under too many times, I won't be able to bring her back.

In the background, I barely hear the commotion that these events always cause. I suspect it is worse than normal considering the circumstances, but I can't risk losing eye contact to find out for sure. None of that matters anyway. Keeping the Verndari woman in the present for as long as possible is my top priority. Our community can't lose her; I can't lose her.

When tall-tail buzz and energy flows around her, I sigh in relief. I let my hands drop from her face, knowing that soon everything would be okay. I watch her in amazement as she looks relaxed for the first time since we've met her. The pain that has been permanently etched on her face is gone and a look of bliss replaces it.

I practically sigh in relief. Those feelings are short lived as seconds later I feel it. The buzz causes me to collapse on the floor. What little control I had, I lose, as the shaking starts, and the burning sensation we all hear about, but usually never experience, starts on my right temple. Fuck!

All Verndari are taught from a young age what a blessing being chosen is. What they neglected to tell you was how painful it was. It feels like I am being burned from the inside out. I don't know how long I lay there; I was oblivious to everything going on around me. As the pain fades, I begin hearing the moans of a few others. When the moaning finally stops, you could have heard a pin drop. I open my eyes to see Ryuu and the others staring at me, shock very much present on their faces. I open my mouth to say some smart-ass comment, when I hear her scream and I'm suddenly pulled in.

I look around, knowing that this differs from the visions I am used to. It is more real than my usual visions. I am standing next to my girl; she has a look of pure dread on her face. She is pleading for someone to help her, but she doesn't think anyone will. Her past has taught her that. I plan to prove her wrong and make sure she knows we will always come to her aid, no matter what.

We are in her room in the human settlement; it's more rundown than I remember. There is a fresh hole in the roof big enough to see the evening sky. The window has been shattered and the glass that remains has sharp jagged edges.

My girl has a shard of glass in her left hand. She is holding it tight enough that I can see blood dripping down her closed palm. I can see her fighting the pull the implanted memories are having on her mind. There is a game of tug-of-war going on in her mind. A game she is getting closer and closer to losing. I watch the glass move closer to her right wrist and then it pulls back slightly. Instantly, I grab a hold of her left wrist, startling her. She looks me right in eyes. "This isn't what you want. I can see it in your eyes. Let me take it away." I tell her, hoping I can get through to her.

In that instant, her grip on the glass loosens and I pull it from her hand and let it fall to the ground. I pull her into my arms in a tight hug. I can feel her as if she were real. "I will let nothing happen to you." I say right before a red glow surrounds her. When I feel the tension in her disappear, I smile with happiness and relief seconds before blackness surrounds me. Her other mates have arrived.

9: ORI

Being in your Mates Arms is Magical

-Ljot

As I look in the stranger's eyes, a tingle comes over me. I suddenly feel no pain and a relief hits me that is pure bliss. It only lasted a minute, but that minute is one I will never forget. After hours of both mental and physical pain, I thought I had no hope left. That pain free minute gave me the hope that I had lost hours ago. The hope I needed to continue fighting.

As if the universe is using this moment as a practical joke, I am pulled into another memory that never was. This time I'm standing in my room holding a shard of glass so tight I can feel the pain in my left hand as if this was really happening. When I feel the glass scrape at my right wrist, I focus all my energy on stopping myself. I never wanted this. I didn't take the abuse for the young kids in the house just to allow it to break me. If anything, it strengthened me and made me more resilient. My heart knows this would never happen of my own volition. I used that certainty to help me focus on trying to stop myself. I didn't even notice the man with the beautiful eyes standing next to me. It isn't until he grabs my left wrist that I can focus on him. He is all that matters. I see his mouth moving, but I don't know what he is saying. When the grip I have on the glass loosens and I hear it clang on the floor, I am pulled into a tight hug.

It feels wonderful and gives me something beautiful to focus on. It's been a long time since I've been hugged. The feeling is so nice that I don't even notice when someone digs in my head and one by one the images, unwanted memories, and unwanted feelings disappear from my mind. I hope I never see or feel them again. They can burn in hell for all I care.

When I feel the last nightmare removed, all I'm left with is the memory of the man with beautiful eyes. I'll cherish this man forever. As the darkness consumes me, my mind battles the dark space that has become a second home. While it is peaceful, I know there won't be any pain when I wake up. I am struggling between staying where it's comfortable and going towards the unknown. I fear living in the real world. A new life awaits me. What's happening to me? Where am I going to go? Where am I going to stay? How am I going to live? Being surrounded by uncertainty scares most people. But the prospect of being able to finally live is too enticing.

I don't know how long I'm in the darkness; I really hope it wasn't long. When I feel the frantic emotions from others around me, I was even more eager to go back. The feelings of sadness and worry pour into me, making me push myself back to reality. Why is everyone so worried?

I smile to myself, elated to find my own emotions. I can tell where my emotions begin, and which emotions are mine. As I catalog all the feelings flowing through me, I count three separate signatures. Why are so many people worried? I question right before my eyes open to my new life.

Surrounding me are three of the most gorgeous men I have ever seen. One of them, in particular, stands out over the others. I would remember his piercing chocolate brown eyes anywhere. He is the man from my memories.

"It's you." I say, unable to keep my eyes off him.

"It's me." He says reaching out and taking me from someone's arms. How did I not realize I was being held? His voice pulls my focus as I hear him say, "Nothing like that will ever happen to you again." He says with such certainty that I believe him. That is the moment I feel the emotions from others quickly change from worry to relief. They're worried about me. No-one has ever been worried about me before.

"What happened?" I ask, trying to distract myself from all the new emotions trying to surface. Emotions that I have kept hidden for a long time... acceptance, love, empowerment, gratitude, worthiness, and hope. If I let them surface, I'll breakdown. I can't let myself breakdown in front of him. So instead of acknowledging my feelings, I glance up at him, waiting for a response. He says nothing at first, so I rest my head on his shoulder. Part of me realizes that I should ask him to put me down, but I am enjoying the feeling of being held too much. Too bad it can't last forever, I think, as I close my eyes.

The movement of his chest makes me realize he is chuckling. "I'll hold you as often as you'll let me." He says. "Now sleep, we'll talk in the morning." I'm about to protest when I feel three consecutive kisses apply to my forehead. A girl could get used to this.

I sigh in contentment as I allow myself to drift off to sleep.

10: CEDRICK

Mates are Precious

-Ljot

Coming out of the vision was a strange sensation. It was like a veil was being lifted, clearing my vision. The first thing I notice is that Dain is still holding my girl; I need to get her name, I think, as I analyze the other men who have joined the party. I know instinctually that these men are her other mates. I didn't need the prominently displayed mating mark to tell me this was the case.

Our mating mark is unique in its multi-colored hue; it matches our mate beautifully. The mating mark appears once our mate's magic links with our own. Each mark is unique to each female and appears on each of her mates in location the bond originates. Mine should be on my temple. The pain a Verndari male feels is the appearance of their mark. I can't wait to see what mine looks like; my mark is something I never thought I'd get the chance to see.

The first Century after the appearance of the Verndari, the linking of our magic happened naturally. After the war, the Council changed our customs and decided that linking of our magic was going to be forced when the female came of age. To them, continuing our line was more important than allowing nature to take its course. The ceremony a Verndari Female goes through is a way to make the forced matings culturally acceptable. The results are not always compatible with the Council's desires. Take tonight's for example, two young Verndari Men have found their mate. It's a rare occurrence for individuals so young. I know plenty of older members in our society that have waited for their entire lives to find their mate. Plenty Verndari don't believe the young deserve to hold the power that comes along with having a mate. These two men have proven themselves tonight as more than capable of handling the power they now possess.

Her other mates stand on either side of Dain. Each one has a hand on my girl's temple. Direct contact with her skin must have been needed for them to remove all those implanted feelings and memories. I will forever be grateful to them both. While they are young, they pulled through and helped our girl when it mattered most. What they accomplished is the first step to helping her heal.

One man is of average height at about 6 foot tall. He has short buzz cut hair that is a vibrant blue, unusual for one of our kind. The other man is short at about 5 foot 7, also unusual for our kind. His bald tattooed head is doing absolutely nothing for his height.

I can sense through our new bond that the two men are appraising me. We only allow ourselves a minute before our focus goes back to our girl. She hasn't stirred yet, which worries me. I reach my hand out caressing her cheek trying to coax her back to us. It takes a moment, but when she finally opens her eyes, I am beyond relieved.

"It's you." She says staring right at me.

"It's me." I confirm as I reach over and pull her from Dain's arms. "Nothing like that will ever happen to you again." I promise. That is one promise I am determined to keep; my heart can't handle seeing her in so much pain.

"What happened?" she asks as she lays her head on my shoulder. I can sense how content she is to be in my arms. "I'll hold you as often as you'll let me." I tell her, loving the feel of having her in my arms; her other mates would hold her anytime as well. If she wants held, all she has to do is ask.

I kiss her forehead and tell her to sleep. I'm sure she is exhausted after everything she has been through today. Her other mates follow suit kissing her lightly on the forehead and within seconds of the last kiss, she is sound asleep in my arms.

"Come on," the blue-haired man says. "They made sure one of the mate suites was cleaned and prepped. We can go there."

I look back at Ryuu because my heart is conflicted. I haven't left my team in decades. They were the ones that pulled me out of my depression. Life without my team is an unknown. The other side of me knows that I could never leave the girl in my arms; she is the center of my world. Ryuu gives me a nod of encouragement. There is no anger or resentment in his eyes. I can see his happiness shining back at me. He would never take this away from me. He knows how important and rare it is. That encouragement is all I needed. With one last look at the men I have called brothers, I follow the blue-haired man out the door.

The mate dorms couldn't have been any further from the hall we were in. We end up climbing two different stairwells and five flights of stairs before we make it to the room. It's in the very back of the building. The dorm room itself is much nicer than what I remembered. The dorm has four primary rooms, a bath, a living area, a small kitchen, and a large bedroom.

Without a second thought, we head straight for the bedroom. I lay our girl down in the center of the gigantic bed. Baldy grabs an afghan and covers our girl. Man... I really need to learn their names.

She is restless at first, so none of us move. We just watch and wait patiently. When she is finally in a peaceful sleep, we depart to the living room. I am the first to leave her in the bedroom. The blue-haired mate is not far behind me. We end up sitting on a sofa and wait patiently for baldy. It takes a little while, but he eventually comes out. Through our new bond, I can sense how hard it was for him to leave her. He only came out because he knows the three of us need to talk... before she wakes up; it is essential that we agree. The transition is going to be difficult for her. No need to make it harder because of ignorance. These men need to know her story. I just hope they handle it well.

11: ORION

Love the Unexpected

-Ljot

I was in the middle of my combat class when the call came in to move to the hall. After they made the announcement, you could've heard a pin drop in the room. They only use the hall for one thing; a female had awakened.

Everyone was shocked. We only have a few female awakenings each year and the mating ceremonies are scheduled in advance; they have to be, when all eligible males are required to attend. Why, you ask? Because it is imperative that a female find her full circle. If anyone is missing from these ceremonies, it's possible for the female to come out of it with an incomplete circle, which is dangerous. When the mating ceremonies were first initiated, a few incomplete circles were created. Each one ended worse than the last. When one female died after her final mate could not be found, the Council finally declared that all un-mated male Verndari must be present for every mating ceremony. They couldn't risk losing more female Verndari.

There haven't been any issues since which ensuring that rule would never be revoked. How they are going to ensure that everyone arrives for a surprise mating ceremony?

That is just one of many questions that goes through my mind as we walk toward the hall. My surrounding classmates are full of excitement; most Verndari men are excited when another opportunity to find our mate arrives. A select few of Verndari gave up on finding a mate a long time ago. For these individuals, going to the ceremonies is an annoyance. Personally, I still held onto hope that I will find her one day.

We are sitting in the hall for about an hour as we watch more and more Verndari arrive. The hall is packed, with the youngest of us standing against the walls and standing on the stairs trying to find room. When the woman enters the room, it's easy to recognize that something is wrong. Instead of walking in, she is being carried in by a Verndari team. One of them appears to be trying to keep her awake. Even from my spot high in the rafters, I can hear the occasional moan and whimper that escapes her. The Council member in charge of the ceremony rushes through the motions of the ceremony. As soon as the last words escape his mouth, I collapse on the floor in front of my seat.

The pain is unlike anything I have ever felt. I clutch my side as the burning sensation increases in strength. It only lasted a minute, but that was one long fucking minute. My hand was still on my side when I hear her screams. I was standing in seconds, the pain no longer mattering. I had to help her, my mate. Ignoring the whispers and stares, I jump over seats and railings, trying to get to her as fast as I can.

About twenty seats to my left, I see Barrett matching my pace, running straight toward our girl. When we reached the bottom of the stadium stairs, the thud of us landing on the ground reverberated throughout the hall. Neither one of us hesitated, we both ran straight for her; she needs us.

While I know our abilities are similar, we rarely work together. Being a grade above me, our interactions are limited. This does not slow us down. As soon as we reach her, we take one second to look at each other. With a nod from Barrett, we both reach out and touch her temples. It is time to fix our girl.

As soon as my hand contacts her temple, I am swept into her abyss of memories and Images. Glancing at the flashes of imagery, I know immediately that fake memories have implanted in her mind. One glace at an image allows me to sense if it is real or fake. Instinctually, I throw that fake Images right towards Barrett. I don't exactly see him; I can just sense him. He is the other comforting presence in the mist of the nightmares. What I see in her mind has me angry. The only thing keeping me from leaving and killing someone is knowing how vital it is to get rid of all the lies. The lies implanted in her head may be bad, but the truth of her life isn't any better. I would do anything to take away all the pain and abuse.

Barrett:

At first, I just feel like I am floating in Chaos. I get seconds to adapt before a ball of memories is shot right at me. I can't see the images; I can only feel the emotions that the memory elicited. What I feel is appalling. I do the first thing that comes naturally; I zap it and watch it disintegrate right in front of my eyes. I really hope she didn't want to keep that memory. I question whether I should feel bad for destroying a memory, but when another comes right at me with the same negative energy, I focus all my power on getting rid of all the terrible memories coming my way. Slowly, one by one, I get rid of them. When the last one has disintegrated, I am pulled back to reality.

Across from me, I see Orion, with anger radiating off him. In that moment, I realized that Orion could see everything. I might not know him well, but his skills are well known amongst our kind. There aren't many Verndari that can peer into minds like he can. He may be a year younger than me, but even I can admit that his power is impressive. If his anger is any indication, those memories I zapped were probably worse than anything I could have imagined.

The next few hours are a blur as we bring our girl to the mated suite. I watch as she is gently laid in bed. She is instantly restless. I would give anything to lay down with her. I want to hold her close and keep the nightmares away. I hold back though, knowing she probably didn't want to wake up to a stranger in her bed. We silently watch and wait. It takes a few hours, but eventually she lays peacefully in bed.

The tension in the room dropped significantly when it finally dawned on all of us that our mate was going to be okay; we'd make sure of it. One by one, we slowly start to make our way out to the living room. The other two men leave before me. I stay just a little longer. I am having a hard time leaving her after seeing her in so much pain earlier; it brought back too many memories. My mother had an incomplete circle. While she survived, she has episodes of pain that we watched her suffer through year after year. She still suffers painful episodes to this day.

The pain my mate was in hit too close to home. I feel my hand rubbing across my face; I'm conflicted. I want to stay with my mate, but I know I need to go join the other men. So, I take one last look at our girl before I walk out. I end up finding them on the couch waiting for me. I hope they didn't mind waiting. When I reach them, I see only understanding in their eyes.

12: MASTER KAI

Magic is a piece of us; without it, we are not whole.

-Ljot

B uzz of unbalance energy has been rippling over my skin since Ori entered our grounds. After the mating ceremony, the buzz should have disappeared. When it didn't, I knew there was something wrong. I went straight to the Council and warned them. While surprised, they didn't seem too worried. The Council insists that their hands are tied, and nothing could be done. Being the stubborn fool that I am, what do I do? I follow the Headmaster back to his office. My appearance didn't surprise him.

"We have to find the remaining mate." I insist as soon as we get within the protection of his office walls. The Headmaster has his back to me and is looking out the window on the far side of his office.

"We do?" He questions me without looking me in the eyes.

"YES! We have to get her powers balanced… it won't end well otherwise." I argue. I'm lucky that the Headmaster is one of the few people who knows the true nature and strength of my powers.

"She'll die, won't she?" He asks rhetorically. I answer him anyway; I'm a bastard like that.

"She has 48 hours at most. You know who was missing. Call them in."

"Of course I do." He starts. "I have argued for years that the missing individuals should be included in the ceremonies, but I get out voted every year. The individuals that were not present are on the Council's shit list. The rest of the Council feels these men don't deserve to find mates." He pushes briefly, making me hold my breath. Does he agree with them? Or is he going to help me save this young woman's life? "Lucky for you," he continues, "I know exactly where they all are and how to get a hold of them."

"How many?" I ask, wondering how many men have been unfortunate enough to piss the Council off.

"Lucky number 13. I will get a hold of their handlers and get them here in the morning. We just have one problem… I don't know how I can convince the other Council members to let her mate stay with her. These men gave up the right to a mate when they took their positions."

"No One FUCKING does that." I insist, unwilling to believe any man would give up their future like that.

He turns towards me and looks me in the eyes for the first time since I entered his office. The Headmaster says nothing, but the look in his eyes tells me one thing. These men didn't give up their rights, their rights were taken from them. FUCK! That complicates things. No more words needed to be exchanged, so I take my leave.

As I'm walking down the halls towards my room, my mind wonders to the ceremony earlier. Most of the student body here doesn't realize how historical the ceremony was today. Her mating ceremony will be part of our history and studied for years to come. Not only was this woman an unknown Verndari, which is a rare occurrence these days, but she was in pain during the mating ceremony. Pain is a common response during an awakening, but that pain should have passed by the time the ceremony started. If you took the opportunity to look at her, you could see the pain and fear etched on her face. It was brutal to watch. Verndari cherish our females and treat them like glass from the time they are born. No Verndari female alive has ever had experiences like this woman. They can't empathize with what she went through.

When the final ceremonial words were spoken, the tension in the room dropped significantly, but only for a second. We all expected her pain to stop with the initiating of the bonds, but it did not fix her problem.

As a teacher, pride fills me as I watched Barrett and Orion's reactions. It was impressive how quickly they responded. It would have been difficult for anyone to react as quickly as they did. Being selected as a mate causes our bodies to reorganize how our magic is structured within us. It is exhausting and painful on its own. The selected mates collapse anywhere from 10 minutes to a few hours. Both Barrett and Orion being able to respond within just minutes of the transition starting just reiterates the gravity of her situation. They knew she needed them and that overpowered their bodies need to shut down.

Barrett and Orion are just coming into adulthood themselves. Did their youth work to their advantage? At their age, you don't really expect to find your mate. Sure, all the students talk about the possibility, but none of them expect that dream to come to fruition at their age. The odds of the selected mates being students is too small. There are too many others of our kind way older than they are that are still waiting for their mate to appear. Many will never find them. It is common for Verndari men to have same-sex relationships; for some, it fills the void of their missing mate.

We all watch and wait as all three mates work to free the Verndari female from the pain she is in. When we finally see a relaxed expression appear on her face, the tension in the room disappears.

I am the only one in the room who can tell she isn't grounded. That is incredibly dangerous for any Verndari Female, but more so for a Verndari that is unfamiliar with our ways. I want to warn all the men of what they will soon be facing, but I can't bring myself to do it. I want them to enjoy this time with her. If the Headmaster doesn't pull through, this may be the only time they have with their mate.

13: CEDRICK

My Mates became Best Friends. Couldn't have asked for anything better.

-Ljot

W e wait patiently for the last of us to leave our girl. He takes a while, but his desire to stay near her is strong. I can sense how difficult it is for him to leave her. It is too early for him to open up to me, but I'd bet this was a trigger for him. Only time will tell.

Both these men have more magical power than regular Verndari. Our physical oddities are signs to other Verndari of the power we hold. Between my white blond hair, the other's bright blue hair, and the bald one, we all hold extra power in different areas. It's a very rare combination to see. There must be a reason we are all mates to the same woman. I am still contemplating our strange dynamic when the last of us walks in.

"Sorry that took me so long." He says as he sits down with us. "I'm Barrett."

"Nice to meet you, Barrett." I say as I openly examine him and the other man.

"Orion." the other man answers simply.

"I'm Cedrick." I say finally giving them my name.

"The Cedrick?" Barrett asks with shock and awe evident in his voice.

"Yup." Nothing like one-word answers. My favorite form of entertainment. They both glance at each other, not quite certain what to say; they obviously want more information from me, but all that personal shit is going to have to wait. Our girl is way more important. "What did the school tell you about this awakening?" I ask them both.

"Nothing." "Diddly-squat." They answer simultaneously. Of course not, I shouldn't have suspected otherwise. The Council has always been hush-hush; there is no way they would want the reality of her situation getting out. It would make them look bad. It would appall most Verndari if they knew the truth of her life.

"I don't know her name. We are going to have to ask her when she wakes, but I suspect she doesn't know what she is." I tell them, needing to get to the heart of the problem.

"How the hell is that possible?" Barrett asks, shocked as hell.

"My team and I rescued her from the human part of society. I suspect she has grown up thinking she was human."

"Humans did all that to her?" Orion asks with pain and anger radiating in his eyes.

"You can see memories." I state directly. I didn't need to hear his answer to know I am right. He would have never asked otherwise. It is the only thing that makes sense.

"Yes" he says, answering my rhetorical question.

"Humans did it all." I answer, understanding just how badly he needed to know for sure. I am just as appalled as he is and want to go slaughter everyone who harmed my girl.

"I want to go kill them all." He says reiterating my thoughts. He has no sympathy in his voice, just pure anger. He balls his hands into fists with his knuckles going white. If any of the humans were present, his look alone would kill them. "You and me both." I tell him. I understand exactly where he is coming from.

"The transition from human society to Verndari is going to be rough for her. Not only does she need to heal because of her shit past, she also needs to learn who she is, who we are to her, and learn the nuances of our society. She didn't grow up like other Verndari woman. It is going to be a big shift for her."

"How bad was it?" Barrett asks, confirming my suspicion that seeing into a person's memories isn't a power he holds.

"Real Bad." "Fucking terrible." Orion and I answer simultaneously. We are silent after that, allowing Barrett time to digest what we are trying to tell him without having to go into the gritty details. It's not my place to tell him. I am hoping our girl opens up to us on her own, but that will take time.

A scream sounds out from the bedroom, causing all three of us to scramble up and out of our chairs. Racing to the bedroom, we see her on the bed tossing and turning. She continues to moan and whimper in what sounds like pain. She is having a nightmare.

"She is reliving something." Orion tells us in a quiet, somber voice, echoing my thoughts.

"I can't take this anymore" Barrett says as he climbs into bed beside her. We all watch as he pulls her close, allowing his arm to rest around her waist. We watch in surprise as she instantly settles down. When I realize she is still a little restless, I look over at Orion and motion my head toward the bed. In the end, I end up on the other side of our girl with my hand resting on her thigh, while Orion lays right next to Barrett, slipping his arm over him so he can hold on to her hand. When all three of us have a hand resting on her, she finally falls back into a peaceful sleep.

14: ORI

There's Fire in my Veins

-Ljot

Images of the three men I got glimpses of are prominent in my dreams. They make me feel as safe in my dreams as they did in real life. I have never felt safe before. It's a strange feeling that I want to keep and never let go of. My feelings of safety dissipate when I wake up. My system jolts as my senses take in my surroundings. There is an unbearable heat surrounding me and the sounds of my own intense whimpers and moans penetrate my ears. Until that instant, I didn't realize how much pain I was in. Seconds later, I feel three different hands on my head, one on my cheek trying to sooth me, one holding the back of my neck, while the last is on my forehead.

"She is boiling up." One of them says with concern clear in his voice.

"You know what that means." Someone else says matter-of-factly, like the answer to my weird heat should be obvious to all of them.

"She is missing someone." The concerned voice states.

The hand holding my neck instantly leaves me. Yelling quickly follows the hands' departure. "WHO THE FUCK WAS MISSING. NO ONE IS ALLOWED TO BE ABSENT."

Remind me to never make him mad. He is undoubtedly pissed off. I can imagine the vein in the middle of his forehead popping out of his head. The image in my head makes me want to chuckle. Unfortunately, it comes out as more of a moan. My laughter makes the heat in my body stir, causing an increase in the pain that is already quickly approaching my breaking point.

"Oh, Baby," someone laying next to me says while pulling me closer. "We will find him. I promise we will find him." His confident words reassure me, even though I don't understand what is happening.

"You can't promise that. We don't even know where to start." Someone says killing all the optimism.

"I can help with that." An unfamiliar voice interjects. I hear a door shut behind him telling me he just entered whatever room I am in. "The only options are the handful of Verndari that the Council placed undercover. They never attend."

"How are we going to get them here?" The person holding me asks with desperation in his voice.

"I have already reached out to all the handlers. They all committed to getting their man here as quick as they can; they understand the urgency."

"Thank You Headmaster." a few men say simultaneously. Headmaster? Am I at a school? I put that information aside for now, as I continue to listen; my brain desperately clinging onto all the information it can. "The first should be here soon." The " Headmaster" states, giving me no useful information.

As I lay there, time passes slowly with the fire and pain in my bones increasing steadily. Occasionally, I feel a few caresses, some on my calf, some on my arms, each caress causing the fire in me to burn more painfully. None of them helping the way those around me are hoping. I can sense the hope of three individuals spike with the arrival of each new individual.

"Cedrick." Someone with a deep gravelly voice says.

"Khalid." The man holding me responds.

"How many others have tried?" the man I now know as Khalid asks.

"You're our last option. I really hope it's you. You're a good man." So… we like this one. I think as seconds later, I feel a strong calloused hand touch my calf just like all the others that came before him. This time, though, the heat in my body instantly cools like I have been put in an ice bath. A sigh in relief escapes me without me even realizing it.

"Thank You." I mumble even though I am not sure I know exactly what I am thanking him for.

15: KHALID

Finding your Mates is a Gift... Cherish it always.

-Ljot

Keeping myself standing during the awakening was difficult. The blast was intense; the individual had to be close. I wanted to run out and help them; this was not the place to have your awakening. Unfortunately, I was in no position to help. I could only hope that someone else would get to them quickly.

I am currently standing in the alley across from my mark's house. I have been watching this same house for days, learning her routines. Like clockwork, she leaves the house. I wait quietly until the click clack of her heels disappears into the night. Putting the hood of my cloak up, I slowly make my way to the house. Like all the houses in Tarengill, it is in disrepair, so it isn't difficult to find a window to slip into. I slowly travel through the house to the office in the back. There are papers scattered everywhere. The first few are your standard financial statements. The amount of money she has is intriguing. With the amount of money she has in the bank, she has no reason to live in this dump. Which means… she is definitely up to something. No sane person would live in Tarengill unless they had too.

I make my way deeper into the office and find a safe hidden in the back behind an old painting. It's the only object in this house in peak condition. I lift my hands up and twist the nob, using my magic to pick the lock; listening intently for the telltale click of the lock. I hit the jackpot when the door swings open. Inside I find photo after photo of all the Council member. She has been a busy girl.

"I thought she was paranoid when she told me she was being watched." Someone says from behind me. I turn around just as a knife is thrown at my head. I easily stop it in mid-air and send it back toward the man who entered. His buff stature tells me he is probably a security guard for her. That won't matter though, as the butt end of the knife hits him right in the head. I intentionally put enough force on the knife that as soon as it hits his forehead, he is out cold. I have at-least five minutes. I gather the photos and quickly head out. I need to get these photos to Lulu, my handler. She has to warn the Council; they have a stalker.

My call to her was quick. I told her I had something big. She said she would meet me at our usual rundown bar the next day. I must watch my back; I can't let anyone get these photos. I stay awake for the next 24 hours knowing it is the only way I can guarantee the safety of these photos.

When it is finally time for the meet, I slip into the bar and grab my usual drink. The bar itself is disgusting, but it helps the people of this area cope with their lives. If it wasn't so important for me to blend in, I wouldn't drink anything from this place. But walking into the bar and not having a drink is a sure way for me to stand out, which is the opposite of what I need at the moment.

My handler, Lulu, is one tough bitch. It doesn't surprise me that she convinced her mates to let her work as a handler. Granted, at least one of them is always close by; they are probably right down the road. We are a very over-protective bunch; being a handler isn't exactly a safe occupation.

She sits down in the stool next to me, ignoring the normal pleasantries that we always exchange. "We need to get you to the academy Khalid." She says as I hand her the photos.

"Whys that?" I question. I haven't been back to the academy since I graduated. Last time I checked… they didn't want me there either.

"The newly awoken was female." She starts. "She is missing a mate." Her voice is calm, but inside she is breaking. She feels for the new woman. Which means it must be bad.

When the Council forced me into this position, I had to give up on finding my mate. I was never allowed to be a part of the ceremonies and most females can live a full life even when missing a mate. This woman must be special. In the past, the Council has not cared that a female Verndari was missing a mate.

"How bad is it?" I ask honestly afraid of the answer.

"She is going to die if we don't find her mate. Her temp has already risen to 125 degrees. She can't hold on much longer. Hell... most of the Council is surprised she held on as long as she has. You are one of only a handful of options left."

"You know I gave up on the idea of a mate a long time ago, Lulu."

"I know that Khalid, but this is your chance. Probably your only chance. Besides... If you found out she was your mate and you let her die. What would you do?"

"Probably kill myself" I respond honestly.

"Follow me out back, we can be there in moments." She says as she heads out the back door. I wait a few moments before following her. The people in this bar may be poor, but they aren't stupid. Hopefully, they think I am about to give her a good fucking; don't need anyone here getting too suspicious.

As soon as I make it out into the alley, I watch as Lulu hands one of her mates the photos and then turns to stare at me with her arms crossed like she knows exactly what I'm thinking. She probably does. She motions for me to follow her to the back of the alley where I find her remaining mates creating a portal. I willingly walk straight for it not stopping till

I have walked all the way through and find myself in a very crowded bedroom.

Three men are laying on the bed surrounding a figure that I assume is the female; they must be her mates. In the center of the room, the Headmaster is pacing. You can see the indent of the path he has created on the floor. On the far side of the room, most of Ryuu's team sits on the floor with somber looks on their faces.

I've worked with their team a few times. They are all honorable men, but I'm surprised to see them here; this isn't their usual thing. My head whips to the bed, suddenly realizing Cedrick is laying on the bed. He must be one of her mates. No wonder his entire team is here. His team is like family; they will support him through this regardless of the outcome.

"Cedrick." I say grabbing his attention. He looks right at me. All his emotions clear on his face. "Khalid" he says. Hope blossoming in his eyes.

"How many others have tried?" I ask him.

"You're our last option." He says. "I really hope it's you; you're a good man, Khalid."

I walk straight for them till I'm standing at the end of the bed. The woman laying down has gorgeous dual colored hair that is spread out around her head. Sweat is coating her hair, giving it a wet look; a sure sign that her body is struggling. Her skin is also coated with beads of sweat that are a red hue, making look like her skin is covered in a rash. Fuck... I hope this works. I don't want to think about all the pain she has been in.

I end up sitting at her feet and gently put my hand on her calf. I had seconds to feel how hot her skin was before the pain started. Pain that I never thought I'd get the chance to feel. I welcomed the pain. It gave me hope that a new life was on the horizon. A life of my choosing, not one that was chosen for me.

16: ORI

The Soothing Feel of a Mate's Touch is like no other

-Ljot

I t was hard to perceive how much time passed. As time passed, I continued to feel hotter until I was boiling up from the inside out. Then the best feeling entered my world. A Strong calloused hand touched my calf, instantly a feeling of ice water washed over me extinguishing the heat that has been dominating my body. My skin cooled and within a few moments I could finally open my eyes.

Looking around the room, I counted eight fairly large males all crowded into the small room. How are they all fitting? Out of the eight, the four sitting on the bed with me held my attention. The man sitting to my right has a short military buzz cut. His hair is a vibrant blue with matching eyes. It is a beautiful combination. The man sitting next to him has a bald head with a tattoo covering most of it. The tattoo is fascinating. It is a paisley pattern with swirls. The center of the tattoo holds a red and silver bird. It's beautiful. The man farthest down the bed has a dark complexion. His crooked nose was broken a few too many times, and he has a scar going down his left eye. His beard covers up the end of the scar, making it impossible to see how bad it really is. He has black hair that is messy and unkept; I ache to brush my hand through his hair. The best part though, are his silver eyes; they just pop. My eyes divert to his hand that is still resting on my calf. It has an identical red and silver bird to the one on the other man's head. Who are these people? Do I know them? I feel like I know them.

"That's Orion, Barrett, and Khalid," the man on my left side says in a voice I recognize. I know that voice. My head quickly whips in his direction. It is the man with the beautiful chocolate brown eyes. This time, though, he has the silver and red bird on his temple. I swear that wasn't there before. Where did it come from?

"I'm Cedrick." He says introducing himself. "What's your name?" He asks. It's a simple question but feels extremely important. I study all four men, and anticipation is clear in all their eyes.

"Ori." I say knowingly accepting this new life that is in front of me.

"We are so happy we found you." Barrett says.

"Sorry I was a little late." Khalid says with regret in his eyes. Looking at him, I saw pain radiating out of him. Why is he in pain? "I should have been here sooner." He admits. "I could have prevented all that pain you were in." How could he have prevented it? He wasn't the cause of my pain. Granted, I didn't know what the cause was, but he didn't hurt me. I couldn't stand the look on his face, so I lean forward and grab ahold of his hand. "It's not your fault. Your here now; that is all that matters."

I was so focused on these four men, that I completely forgot about the other four men in the room. The oldest is now standing at the end of the bed with a puzzled look on his face. "How did you end up with the human's Ori? And why the hell didn't we know about you?" He questions me. Am I being interrogated? It feels like an interrogation. Well Fuck him.

"What the hell is wrong with you. Have you seen what she has been through these last couple of days? We almost lost her. If she died, it would have been your fault. Now instead of being happy that she is alive and well, you interrogate her like she is a criminal. I thought you were on our side. Get the FUCK out of our room." He yells fuming. Cedrick is pissed, his entire body is vibrating with rage.

"I am on your side, but it's not that simple. I can't leave until Khalid and the others leave." The man says.

"Khalid isn't leaving." I say with the strength that I learned to use throughout my years in foster care. "He is staying right here."

"He gave up his right to a mate. He leaves now." The older man insists, obviously trying to exert his power.

At that statement, Khalid's hand slips out of mine as he turns and looks right at him, determination suddenly plastered on his face. "Your

Council forced me into this position. It was not a position of choice. I didn't give up my chances of finding a mate, you took it from me. So, if you think for one second that I am going to let you keep her from me now that I have found her, you are crazier than the others on the Council."

"You say you are on our side, but you are trying to force two mates apart. You know what that can do. Why bring them together, just to tear them apart." A man behind him says. This man is tall, definitely over 6 feet. His posture and demeanor display his lack of intimidation. I suspect that extraordinarily little scares him. Glancing over at Cedrick, who now has a smirk on his face, it's easy to determine that we like the new guy.

"You know I am always on your side, Ryuu, but his job does not allow for him to have a mate. Even I can't change that." He says. "I wouldn't force him away if I didn't have to."

"Then give him a different job."

"It's not that simple Ryuu." The older man continues.

"Sure it is... people get new jobs all the time, right? My foster parents got new jobs all the time. Why would Khalid be any different?" I question.

Ryuu smirks at my statement before he continues. "Ori has a point. People get new jobs all the time. Khalid can work with our team. Now there isn't a problem. Why don't you let them be for tonight and they will come by your office in the morning to figure out the rest."

The older man gets a strange look on his face. Surprise maybe. To be honest, I can't decide if he is happy about this or not. "Come by at 0900… but come with a plan. The others Council members will not be easy to persuade." I watch as he takes his leave, heading for the door.

I don't know why I am calling him an old man. He looks to be about the same age as my foster father, but in much better shape. Probably 45 years old at most. That isn't that old. Well… it is old for humans, but these individuals aren't human.

I watch the old man till he stops at the door and looks back towards Ryuu. Ryuu must take that as his cue. He comes closer, talking briefly with Cedrick before heading out with the other two men that were with him. All four men head out, closing the door behind them.

When I am finally left with just my men, I instantly sigh in relief. The tension I was holding leaves my body and is replaced with a sense of contentment. I feel at ease with these four men. It's like I finally arrived home for the very first time.

17: ORI

If someone tries to kill you, know that you are meant for great things.

-Ljot

All four men end up curled around me on the bed I was lying on. I knew I should probably protest, but I was too tired. Besides, it felt nice having them around me. I feel safe for the first time in my life. A feeling I was not ready to give up.

The next morning, Cedrick roused me from my sleep. The others had already gotten up and, by the smell of things, were making breakfast. I learned quickly that Barrett is an excellent cook. He made eggs in a basket and sides of bacon for all of us. I haven't had a warm home cooked breakfast in a long time. A girl could get used to this. With any luck, he will spoil me with breakfast each morning.

As we all sit around the table eating, it is a comfortable silence; It feels like we have all known each other our entire lives. The silence doesn't break until the last of us finishes their meal.

"It's time for our meeting." Cedrick reminds us as we stand from the table. I don't understand what is going on or what is happening to me, but I trust these men. More than I have ever trusted anyone in my life.

Orion walks around the table and grabs my hand. "Come on." He says as he leads me out of our rooms. My eyes roam everywhere as it is my first time out since waking. The halls are built of stone, with windows high enough that the sun is just now peeking into them. The hallways themselves start off dead, but as we make a few turns, more and more individuals appear. Everyone we pass looks in our direction and whispers amongst themselves. It doesn't take a genius to know that they are talking about me.

"Ignore them. They are simply curious." Orion says from next to me.

"Staring is rude." I mumble as I continue to follow my men. My statement did not go unnoticed as all the guys chuckle at my statement.

"We don't get new people here, Ori." Barrett explains. "We have all grown up together, so you are sort of an anomaly. They will get used to you being here and the staring will stop. Don't be too hard on them."

Our walk brings us to a set of beautifully carved wooden doors. The scene carved into the doors is unfamiliar to me. In the center stands a beautiful woman surrounded by four men. I get the impression that there is a deeper meaning to the scene displayed. I am about to ask, when the doors are opened by the older man from last night. He motions for us to enter. Straight ahead is his desk. It is massive and made of wood. Standing next to the monstrosity are two others. They are both wearing decorative robes that I am assuming reflects their station. I take my time analyzing them and quickly determine that the woman is the most calculating. The men feel resentment and anger; it's clear they don't like me. The woman though is suspicious.

"What is Khalid still doing here?" The man next to her asks with disgust.

"I have a new position with Ryuu's team. It gives me the right to stay with my mate." Khalid says from behind me. I can sense his anger, but he is keeping it contained. These people have wronged him in the past.

"After what you have done, you really think she is going to want to keep you? No sane woman would want you as a mate." The woman sneers; anger prominent in her voice. Behind me, I can feel Khalid flinching; her words cut him deep. My head snaps in his direction when I feel him agreeing with her. If he hadn't come for me, I would be dead; deep down, I know that. So, I do the one thing that comes naturally… I snap.

"He is mine and is not going anywhere." I practically yell in anger at the woman. She suddenly laughs and slowly approaches me, like a lion on a hunt.

"You don't even know what you are. You don't know the implications of keeping a man like him as a mate. You should trust your elder's sweetheart." she says putting a fake smile on her face. Does she really think I am going to trust her?

"I think I will trust my instincts and keep him, but thanks." My instincts are telling me not to let him go, so I don't intend on letting him go. I trust my gut. It has always gotten me through the tough times in life. It never once failed me. I doubt it is failing me now.

"If you insist. I will enjoy watching you guys fail." She steps back towards the Headmaster and other men. We stand there watching as they have a discussion which quickly gets heated, if their hand gestures are any indication.

"If they fail, it's on you." the woman directs at the Headmaster, no longer trying to keep up her cheerful facade. We watch as she storms out of the room with the other men in robes hot on her heels. When the door slams shut, my reaction to them can't be contained any longer.

"I don't like them." I state bluntly making the whole room laugh.

"No one does." Barrett says, followed by another chuckle.

"I realize the last few days have been rough, but we have some things to discuss. We can't wait any longer." the Headmaster says with sympathy in his voice. "What do you know about your biological family?"

"Nothing." I tell him honestly. "I've been in foster care since I was born. My parents gave me up.

They didn't want me." I try to keep the pain out of my voice but fail miserably.

"I suspect there is more to the story. We don't give up our children, especially a female. There have been a few occasions where a different family raised a child, but they have always stayed with our own kind. It dangerous to grow up around humans, as I'm sure you have figured out."

"So… I'm not human?" I question, needing to hear it with my own ears.

"No… you are not human. You are a Verndari."

"Holy FUCK!" I say, shocked. Don't get me wrong, I suspected that I was a little different, but a Verndari … never came to mind.

"Surely you suspected something?" the Headmaster asks.

"Sure… I knew I was different. If I wasn't different, then I was Crazy. I was hoping for the former. But I never once suspected that I could be Verndari. I have never seen a female Verndari. Most humans think they are a myth."

"They are rare and precious. When a female Verndari comes of age they are matched with their mates. Their mates help ground their powers. Without them, a female Verndari is sure to perish." He says with a somber voice. "We never enjoy seeing that happen."

"So… these men…" I start as I glance around at the four men that have been by my side since I turned 18.

"Are your mates." He finishes for me. "They are yours. To them, being your mate is an honor. It's an honor to be chosen as a mate; most Verndari men dream of finding their mate only to never see their dream come to fruition."

Part of me Cringes. "I am dependent on them?" I ask. I'm not dependent on anyone.

"On the contrary, they depend on you." He says. His statement shocks me to the core and honestly doesn't make much sense with what little I know about the Verndari. Questions of all kinds jump around in my head, but I'm not sure I can tolerate much more.

"What now?" I ask, not understanding and completely unsure of where all this is ultimately leading.

"As your relationship with them grows, their power gets bound to you. Without you they wouldn't be a Verndari." He states like that statement is normal. "Now that you are matched with your mates, the five of you are going to take specialized classes. Then, in a few months' time, you will take part in a trial. It is vital that you pass the trial." he states suddenly getting profoundly serious.

"Do I want to know what happens if I don't pass?" I question. I look around at my guys as I ask the question; they all have solemn looks on their faces. Yup... probably don't want to know. Too bad the question already came out of my nosy mouth.

"They break the mating bond; females don't live through a break." He says. I gasp, unable to hold my reaction in.

"Why the HELL would you break a bond if the female perishes? You surely do not have enough females to consider that kind of action." I am practically shouting by the time I am done with my mini rant.

"If you don't pass, it means your magic is unstable. That is dangerous for everyone."

FUCK MY LIFE. Can't I just go one day without a death threat? Apparently not.

18: CEDRICK

Silence is Peaceful

-Ljot

O ur Mate has been quiet for the entire afternoon. We got back around lunchtime. As soon as we entered our new home, we watched her as she rushed around the kitchen grabbing something to eat, then scurried with it to the bedroom. She clearly needed a minute to herself, so we gave her the time she needed. None of us want to push her, but we are all worried. The past few days have been a lot for her. A weaker man would have cracked by now. I am proud of how patient we are being, but how long do we give her?

After a few hours of leaving her in peace, I get voted in as the chump who gets to check on her. Why me? I apparently have the strongest connection with her. They aren't wrong. The time we shared in her memories connects us in a unique way.

Even with our connection, there are two ways that this could go. I will either get bonus points for checking in on her… or I will get a shoe thrown at my head. I am hoping it's the first option. I hope I don't fuck this up.

When I make it to the bedroom door, I just stare at it hoping it will just magically open. I end up standing there like an idiot for at least five minutes, possibly more, before I get up the nerve to knock. Stupid, I know.

"Come in," She says from the other side of the door like she was expecting me the entire time. "I was wondering how long it would take you." She states with amusement lacing her voice. Inside the room, I see her sitting cross-legged on the bed. She looks at me with a twinkle in her eye that I haven't seen before. "I knew one of you would come, but I expected it to be sooner."

"We didn't want to push you. After everything you have been through, we suspected you just needed some time. We were trying to respect your need for space, but we are all worried about you." I tell her honestly as I walk further into the room.

"It's a lot to take in." She admits causing the twinkle in her eyes to leave. I watch her as she drops her head, keeping it downcast, while her shoulders droop. I keep my eyes on her as I walk towards the bed and carefully sit next to her. I reach out and grab her hand. She looks up at me in that moment, teary-eyed. I bet it has been a long time since she has let herself cry.

"You are in control of everything, Ori. Nothing needs to be rushed." I say, trying to reassure her.

"I don't want to die." She says as tears fall. And here I thought having four mates had her freaked out. "I didn't go through the hell I did growing up just to die here." She continues adamantly. "But what if I can't do it, and I die anyway?" she asks.

Initially, I am stunned into silence. This strong, powerful woman thinks she is going to fail. I don't think it's possible for a woman as strong as her to fail; especially when her life is on the line. Besides, none of us would let that happen; she already means too much to us... We can't lose her.

I reassure her as best as I can before switching topics. I couldn't stop myself from asking her how she felt about us. I probably should have waited, but I am a nosy bastard sometimes. The tension she was holding in her slips away as she gives a soft laugh behind her tear-stained face.

"You four make me feel safe. I've never had that before." She says making me smile at her admission. She will always be safe with us. I tell her as much as I reach up and caress her cheek.

"Could you guys sleep in here with me tonight?" she suddenly asks, causing a blush to come to her cheeks. I love seeing my woman blush.

"Thank FUCK!" I exclaim, causing her to laugh. "We all assumed we would be sleeping on the floor." She laughs even harder. The sound is magical; I can't wait to hear it more.

"Not tonight. But I will keep the floor as an option if any of you end up in the doghouse." Her response comes out of nowhere, causing a belly laugh to escape from me; I couldn't stop myself if I tried. I haven't laughed that hard in a long time.

"Duly noted." I say, still smiling. "Let me go get the other guys."

Before leaving, I wait a moment, giving her one last chance to back out. When she nods her head at me, I take that as my cue and head towards the living room where I know her other mates will be eagerly waiting.

I'm still smirking when I arrive. Their surprise at the outcome of my conversation with her is inevitable. I know I didn't expect it… so I doubt they would have. Considering recent events, this is the best outcome any of us could have expected.

19 ORI:

Your Mates are the Missing pieces to your Heart!

-Ljot

I have been in the bedroom alone for hours. It's a beautiful room, decorated in purples and blacks. While it definitely has a feminine touch to it. Would my guys be comfortable here?

I thought I needed sometime alone to think. But as more time passes, I find myself glancing towards the door, wanting my men to be here. My men... What a strange concept. How would a relationship with four guys work? Am I even able to let someone in after the life I have lived? I spent so much of my life just trying to survive that the concept of having someone with me is scary. What is even scarier? I want them with me; I'm tired of being alone.

A smile graces my lips when I sense Cedrick on the other side of the door. His nerves are radiating at me, making me smile. He's nervous. He just stands there for so long I'm afraid that he is going to leave. When he finally comes in, I am relieved. Just seeing him lifted all the pressure and stress I had been feeling right off my shoulders. Looking at him, all I wanted was to be held in his muscular arms. But how do I ask? It is so simple, yet so difficult all at the same time. But it's not just Cedrick that I need; I need my other men too. When Cedrick's hand reaches up and strokes my cheek, I finally just spit out my question. I want them all with me.

The exchange is quite comical, which lightens the mood considerably. As he laughs, his whole face lights up; it's like I just gave him a precious gift. When he gets up to get the others, he hesitates for a second; he is giving me a chance to change my mind. I smile reassuringly as him, knowing that I won't ever take back my request. My eyes stay glued to him as he finally leaves. It is the first time that I am allowing myself to enjoy the view. And you know what? That man has a nice ass.

In no time, all four men come scrambling into the room like fire was lit under their asses. My laughter being the only sound resonating throughout the room. I can't stop smiling at them as I wait. Orion is the first to approach me.

"Scoot to the center, sweetheart. Are you going to make room for us?" He questions. I nod my head and move to the center, keeping my eyes on them. To my surprise, they all start stripping. A polite person would have turned away, looked down, something. I am apparently not a polite person. Cause what do I do? I watch every delicious moment. Can you really blame me?

Surprisingly, most of the guys wear boxer briefs. Barrett is the only one in the old-fashioned boxers. They looked good on him. They rested on his hips and gave me a magnificent view of his V cut. I have been swooning over that muscle since my hormones kicked in. I will gladly enjoy that view as often as he lets me.

"See something you like?" Barrett asks with a smirk.

"Maybe." I admit with a grin, unable to take my eyes off him.

"Honey, you can look at any of us like that anytime you want." Khalid says from the foot of the bed. I take my time taking him in. His boxer briefs are black, which doesn't surprise me. He doesn't seem like the type to own too much color. I wonder how long it will take me to introduce a little color into his life?

"You going to change into something more comfortable?" Cedrick asks.

"I don't have anything else." I admit, unable to keep the pain of that fact from reflecting in my voice.

"We fixed that." Orion admits. I watch him go towards one of the two dressers in the room. I must fight to hold in my laughter as I take in his strange underwear. They are a weird mix match of science and math. With bright colors and equations like $E=MC^2$, $A^2 + B^2 = C^2$, and $Pi = 3.1415926...$ They are so in your face that I can't even enjoy the view. What the hell? I didn't expect that from a man that looks like him.

"He really likes math and science." Barrett whispers to me, just in case I didn't figure that out on my own.

"Thanks, Orion." I say as I catch the pale-yellow nightgown being thrown at me. To my surprise, the guys all turn around and give me a little privacy. Now I feel a little bad for watching them strip. I quickly strip down to my underwear and only hesitate for a moment before I remove my bra and panties too. Who wants to stay in three-day-old panties? Not this woman.

When I slip the nightgown on, I instantly smile. This is probably the nicest thing I have ever worn. It's made of a silky material that feels like heaven on my skin. Currently sitting on my heels, the dress is pooling mid-thigh.

"Beautiful." Barrett says as he pulls the blankets down and we both slide under the covers. He quickly puts his arm around my waist and pulls me tightly to his chest. I gasp as I feel the hard length of his cock pressing against my upper thigh.

"Don't worry, it's all for you." Barrett says as Cedrick climbs in and cuddles up close so that his chest is at my back.

"Mine too!" He says from behind me. I can imagine the smirk on his face as he lightly grinds his hard cock against my leg. I was so distracted that I didn't even notice Khalid and Orion climb into bed on either side of Barrett and Cedrick.

The last thing I remember before drifting off to sleep was thinking how safe I felt between my four men.

20: MASTER KAI

Why did I have to be the first?

-Ljot

I haven't slept much these past few days. The chaotic buzz of the young Verndari Woman's power has been bouncing around me. The imbalance is very unsettling. I worried about her and her men; her power was strong enough that she needed all her mates to be properly grounded. I am relieved when I finally feel her power settling. The buzz disappears, and a sense of peace settled in my bones that had been missing.

Closing my eyes, I focus on her energy signature; I now know it quite well. Her energy flowed through her veins smoothly now, but at about five times the concentration of any other Verndari I have met. I knew she was powerful, but her power is even more apparent now. In our society, the power she holds is dangerous. I sense a fight in her future. I hope she is ready.

I'm sitting in my study enjoying my newfound peace when the Headmaster enters. It doesn't surprise me; he often comes to me in times of stress.

The dark shadows under his eyes signal not only his stress but also the toll his body has taken over the last few days. He walks over to the bookshelves that I filled from top to bottom with books, most of which are historical accounts of our people. He immediately goes to the third shelf up, pulling out the perfect book to remove the brandy and glasses that I have hidden behind them.

"How long have you known about my stash?" I ask, smirking. I had thought it was the one secret I still held close. I should have known better; you can't keep anything from the Headmaster.

"60 years." He pauses as if contemplating his thoughts. "I didn't need it till now." He finally admits as he walks to the leather chair sitting next to mine.

"How is she?" I ask as he pours us both a glass.

"Calm for now. The Council won't like who her mate is." He says with a grim expression on his face.

"Who?" I ask.

"Khalid."

"Fuck... Really?!" He just nods his head at me.

Khalid is a wonderful man, but he made one mistake as a young Verndari that the Council still holds against him. It resulted in the death of 8 of our brightest Verndari; one of which was a councilman's son. He has been punished ever since then. He is not kidding that they are not going to like it. A lightbulb instantly goes off in my head. It's more than just Khalid that they are not going to like. "You know what that means?"

I shouldn't have even asked. Of course, the Headmaster knows what that means.

"She has a mate from all four focuses." He says right before he downs a full glass of brandy.

The focuses are the source and center of our power. A Verndari's focus is either the mind, heart, gut/natural instincts, or spirit. Typically, a female's mates are all from the same focus. Occasionally you might find two focuses together, but even that is rare. To this day, I only know of one person who has ever had a mate from all four focuses, Ljot... the original.

As a child, we all hear about the first Awakening; it is the beginning of our history and vital for all Verndari. It happened during a time when humans ruled. In a tiny village, a young woman, Ljot, known to be the outcast of the area, was turning 18. She lived in a small hut on the very outskirts of town. She differed from the others in town; people feared her, never understanding why. Their fear kept her separate from the others in the village. It was a lonely existence that she wanted no part of. For years she planned her escape from that life. Her 18th birthday seemed like an outstanding day to start anew.

During the twilight hours, she left home and started her trek into the unknown. At the exact hour of her birth, a surge of power blasted out of her so intense even the humans felt it. The surge's white light was so bright that it lit up the night's sky. Her power traveled for hundreds of miles before it died out.

From the moment the humans realized the strength of her power, they feared her. Many believe that no individual should ever have that kind of power; they fear what they don't understand. She spent most of her life trying to win people over. She tried to show people that power does not equal malice. She wanted people to remember her as the kind, empathetic individual she was. While many accounts of her kindness exist, those actions were not enough for some individuals. Many were never swayed, fearing her until her death.

It is rumored that she was never at peace, always looking over her shoulder, waiting for the next battle. It took a toll on her, like it would for anybody. The day of her death was the one and only day she was truly at peace. I suspect she knew eternity with her mates was on the horizon; they passed within hours of her passing.

All Verndari know of the strong bond they had. Bonds like theirs are rare these days. I pray that our newest addition will share the same type of bond; she is going to need the strength that it provides.

"Does the Council know?" I ask him before I chug my own brandy.

"No... I can't put it off much longer either. As soon as they figure it out, they will know that she will be more powerful than any of them. They aren't going to like it. Too many of them are power hungry."

I scoff at that. I couldn't have said it any better myself. Most on the Council thrive off the power the position gives them. It's sickening.

"What are you going to do?" I question as I pour us both a second drink.

"Protect her for as long as I can."

Sitting in silence, we quietly continue to drink my brandy. It's rare that we get days like this. Before long, the bottle is empty, and the Headmaster promises to buy me a replacement bottle. I just laugh at him and tell him it isn't necessary. Apparently, he doesn't know about the other bottle stashed on the very bottom shelf. Maybe I can keep a secret from him.

21: ORI

Gaining my Magic changed the path of my Life.

-Ljot

This is ridiculous, I think as I look at my reflection in the mirror. They really make us wear this crap? I'll be honest, when I was told we were taking classes, I wasn't expecting a uniform. I have never had to wear a uniform, and honestly, I don't want to start now. I am used to wearing baggier clothes, sweats, t-shirts, anything that I can be comfortable in. This is the exact opposite of that. The grey and purple pinstripe skirt comes down to my mid-thigh. It's way shorter than I would like and shows off more skin than I'm used to. I'm sure the guys don't mind, but I would much rather be wearing anything else.

They pair the skirt with a shirt that reminds me of a workout gear… it's a silky material that feels smooth against my skin; so at least I have that working for me. The symbol of the school, at least that is what I assume it is, is sown into the lavender shirt and sits on my left breast. The symbol is intriguing. It looks like a tree that is morphing into a phoenix. Wrapped around the symbol is a whip. Altogether, the shirt isn't too bad.

"Why the face?" Khalid asks from behind me as he grabs onto my hips.

"I hate skirts." I admit as I scrunch up my face in disgust. I feel Cedrick's hand suddenly come up to my forehead, trying to smooth out the wrinkles that have formed there. When did he get here?

"I love the way you look in them." Barrett begins. "I could get used to seeing your legs every day." The look in his eyes tells me he wants to see more than just my legs. I feel the blush forming on my face before I can stop it.

"We are going to be late." Orion says from behind me. The distress in his voice is clear. I turn around and see him standing by the door, his feet bouncing up and down displaying his anxiousness. He is wayyyy past ready to be out of here. "He has never been late to class, has he?"

"No." Barrett says from next to me, chuckling his response. "You picked up on that real quick."

"Kind of hard to miss." I whisper to him as we follow Orion out of our rooms. I learned quickly that Orion is the bookworm of my men. It's easy to tease him about it, but secretly I love that about him.

"I heard that." Orion grumbles from the front, causing us all to laugh.

Our first class is in a large room not too far away from our accommodations. It reminded me of a big gymnasium. The ceilings throughout the space are at least twenty feet tall. The wood floor has a waxy look to it that reminds me of an old gymnasium. The inside is devoid of the bleachers and basketball hoops I expected creating a large open area. The wall on the far side of the classroom has targets of various sizes and heights hanging up. At the very front of the classroom, long tables line the wall. As we walk closer, I see bracelets, necklaces, clips, pocket watches as well as bows, swords, machetes, and daggers lined up. The variety of stuff on the table was shocking. What the hell is all that for?

"She's clueless." I hear someone whisper. Looking up, I see two other Verndari females. They are wearing the same thing as me, but have on heels, as opposed to my tennis shoes. They have perfectly manicured nails and have on enough make-up to hide their true appearance. I bet very few individuals know what their actual face looks like.

One of them has on a simple bracelet similar to a few laying on the table. The bracelet has a subtle look to it which opposes the bold look her and her partner in crime give off. I would have assumed she would have worn a bold, in your face accessory. Like the other woman, who's wearing a necklace with an enormous bright blue jewel; the jewel is approximately the size of my fist. You couldn't miss it even if you wanted to; just what I would expect from someone like them.

Before I could retaliate to their clear taunting, the doors behind us open and in walks five men. They all go to the two women in question and I can hear them telling the girls to be nice. I have dealt with their types before. These women have no intention of ever being nice; it won't matter what their men say.

Their interactions between the seven of them tell me a lot. One of the girls has two mates, while the other has three. Based on the familiarity of their interactions, I suspect that these two women have been friends for a long time. It's common knowledge that there aren't many Verndari Woman. I can't help but wonder.... Do all the women know each other? If so, I doubt that will work to my benefit. The woman will have bonded throughout childhood. A bond like that is hard to break into. That fucking sucks.

"Be nice Cora and Lillia." Someone suddenly scolds from the front of the room. My head whips towards the voice. I find an older man standing behind the tables I was perusing earlier. When did he get here? I internally question. The man up front appears to be a similar age to the Headmaster. His hair is a mix of black and grey, giving him a nice salt and pepper look. His eyes are a bright green with a sternness in them that tells me not to fuck with him... duly noted. While everyone else in the room is wearing the school uniform, he is wearing all black with a trench coat. His powerful aura tells me he is probably a teacher.

"My name is Master Kai. I am one of your instructors. In this class, you will learn how to focus your energy. The first step is finding your talisman. For most Verndari Females, the talisman is tradition, but not unnecessary. Most Verndari woman use their talisman as a vessel to hold a little extra magic; I've been told it gives many a sense of security. Ori, you are a little different." Of course I am, I think, as he continues. "Your mates have different focuses making a talisman a necessity. Without it, your energy won't know where to go and could ultimately cause more damage to you or those around you." I listened to him intently, but ultimately did not understand a word of what he just said. I glance over at Orion, the bookworm of my men, and the look on his face promises me an explanation later. He better, I hate being confused.

"Now go find your talisman." He directs waving his hands over the tables like the request he made is simple.

"How am I supposed to know which one to pick?" I ask, even though it sounds like a stupid question.

"You'll know it when you find it." Master Kai says cryptically.

With that, I slowly approach the table. I quickly pass over all the jewelry; none of it even looks appealing. When I get to the weapons, I slowly peruse them. The knives and machetes are too big and bulky for me. There are a couple tempting daggers, but nothing like the whip sitting at the very end of the furthest table. There is only one of them. The whip is a beautiful silver color, and I can't stop myself from reaching out. When I get within an inch, an electric zip comes out of my fingers and straight to the whip.

"And we have a winner." Master Kai says from behind me as I pick it up. "Keep it with you at all times." He says as he hands me a holder for the whip. I wrap it around my hips before securing the whip in place. I glance down at my new accessory and immediately notice how far down my thighs it goes, even when it's wound up. I really need to be able to wear fucking pants. Is that too hard to ask?

22: CEDRICK

A Talisman is the Verndari Woman's Best Friend

-Ljot

S hit... I should have gone over at least the basic expectation, I think, as we enter the training room. We didn't think it was necessary at the time; the four of us didn't want to overwhelm her. But with how the other females were acting, we quickly realized the mistake we made. There are two types of talismans: jewels and weapons. The talisman type picked by the female guides the rest of their lives. When a female picks a jewel, the female and her mates work as store owners, journalists, or any job where the female is safely tucked behind a desk. When a female selects a weapon, the female and her mates are placed with police force, spy, military... pretty much all the dangerous jobs. Those jobs aren't what anyone would want their mate to be a part of.

None of us worried too much until now. Every female in the last millennium has chosen a jewel. So why would Ori be any different? It was stupid to assume she would be like the other Verndari. She isn't a spoiled brat like most of our females. She is a fighter, so it shouldn't surprise me when she quickly walks right by all the jewels. She has absolutely no interest in any of them. She takes her time on the weapons, though.

The more time she spends looking at the weapons, the more I am cursing myself now for my earlier decision; I should have told her the difference between the two. Her other three mates have the same expression of shock on their faces as I feel. She doesn't understand the position she would be putting herself in if she selects a weapon. Then again... we are taught that the pull of a woman's talisman is undeniable. In theory, knowing would not have changed the outcome?

She walks along the full length of the table and stops at the very end. Even from here, the dust that has settled over all the weapons is visible. The further down the table you look, the thicker the dust gets. When she reached the end, I was hoping she would turn back, but instead, she reaches out and within seconds you see the telltale electric spark that signifies a talisman finding its match. She lifts it up and lets the end drop to the floor. The silver whip glows with her red energy; it pulses content to have finally found a home.

Ori smiles as her magical energy settles. Her smile lasted only a few seconds at best, giving me the distinct impression that smiling is a foreign concept for her. I suddenly make it my mission to make her smile every day. I love seeing her smile grace her face.

The entire room is quiet as our instructor gives her the basic talisman knowledge… keep the talisman with you at all times. When she finally walks back over to us, I can't help but tell her the best part about picking a weapon. If this morning is any indication, she is going to be ecstatic. I can't wait to tell her the news.

"You know the best part of having the whip?" I ask her. She shakes her head at me. "You get to wear pants."

"FUCK YEAH!" she screams, the sound echoing off the walls. We all chuckle at her response. "When can I go change?" She asks seriously.

"Ori" Master Kai tries to scold, but even he is hiding a smirk on his face. "You can change after lunch." She quickly gets a pout on her face that makes us all laugh even harder. Well, everyone except the two other girls; they are too uptight to appreciate the humor of the situation. They have had permanent scowls on their faces since we have arrived; I think they were born that way.

"That's three hours away." She says whining. You can tell from the emphasis that graces her whiny voice, that it is all for show. She is trying to manipulate Master Kai into letting her change earlier.

"You can live in a skirt for three hours. It won't kill you." Master Kai says with his signature straight face.

"I'm not so sure." She grumbles under her breath. Master Kai looks at her with his signature glare, effectively shutting her up. Most students end up on the receiving end of his glares at one point or another. It is the only warning you get. She was smart to shut up.

"This is important… especially for you, Ori" He says looking right at her. "And it is always good to get a reminder." He says turning towards Cora and Lillia daring them to question him. I am not surprised when I see them both roll their eyes; it's not the first time we have seen those eye rolls. I would never stand for that kind of rude behavior, even from our mate. If the looks on their mate's faces is any indication, they feel the same way. I suspect that Cora and Lillia are going to get a talking to later. The big question though is whether their mate's words are going to have any effect on them.

"The Talisman…" Kai begins, bringing our attention back to him "is a tradition that we have honored for centuries. Our females get one Talisman in their lives, and we teach them from an early age to respect and protect their Talisman. For most Verndari females, like Cora and Lillia, a talisman is not a necessity. They can safely perform their magic without it. Why? Their mates all have the same focus. For you, Ori," Master Kai starts to explain, turning to look right at her. He needs to ensure she understands the gravity of her situation. "Your talisman is more than just tradition. It is a necessity. Having mates from multiple focuses can make your magic flare dangerously, especially when it doesn't know where to go. Your talisman will ground all four magical focuses in one place. Take it with you everywhere.

Sleep with it. It needs to become an extension of your body." Ori gulps and nods her head.

I think he got his point across; Ori is going to have that whip glued to her. I can sense her fear from here. I don't think he meant to scare her, but he succeeded. While he could have broken the news to her more gracefully, Master Kai has never been a graceful man. He continues by telling us our schedules not even fazed by her reaction; he can also be an unemphatic bastard at times.

After this class, we have chemistry and history. Basic classes for most of us, but it will be difficult for Ori to catch up. Being raised with the humans means she knows next to nothing. Verndari Chemistry is the study of the make-up of our magic; Verndari been taught the information since we were kids. It's an easy class for us but will be a challenge for her; The information though will be vital for her to understand who she really is and how to handle her magic. History is exactly as it sounds; it is the history of our kind. Let's be honest... she will be bored in that class. But after that is lunch before we head to our specialized classes.

He informs Ori that her classes will be separate from Cora and Lillia as they have jewels, and she has a weapon. She doesn't seem upset about that, but I can see the questions flashing across her face. She doesn't ask them, yet, but I'm sure she will ask them all later. I'll stay up all night and answer all her questions she has if she needs me too.

23: RYUU

Appreciate your Unique Qualities

-Ljot

The Headmaster called us to his office as soon as the talisman selection was over. While I anticipated the current conversation, both Kai and the Headmaster seem surprised by today's events. How are they shocked? She has gone against all our stereotypes. Why would this be any different?

Kai is currently telling the Headmaster about Ori's Talisman selection. Kai leaves no details out as he explains Ori's weapon selection, which is unheard of these days. It has been almost a millennium since a Verndari female selected a weapon.

"There is no one to train her." The Headmaster grumbles for the hundredth time. Does he think repeating this will change the current situation? "Why did you even give her the option of selecting a weapon?" He asks. His question is absurd, and he knows it. You can't limit the female's choice of talismans. A talisman selects the female just as much as the female selects it. It is a bond unique to the

Verndari female. The Council had to have realized someone would have selected a weapon eventually.

"She has had to fight her entire life. Does it really surprise you that a weapon called to her?" I ask honestly. "Because it shouldn't. It is what I expected. We haven't coddled her like our other females." The Headmaster looks over at me with an inquisitive expression on his face. I don't think he put the puzzle pieces together like that before.

"You're right, Ryuu. I should have expected it, but what do I do. There is no one to teach her." He says. This time, though, he sounds lost. The Headmaster genuinely enjoys helping all students grow into their powers. He can't do right by her if there is no one to teach her.

"My team and I will teach her." I state simply. To me, it makes sense to have a team like us work with her. We at least have the combat training to teach her the basics.

"How?" He asks, knowing we know jack about how weapon talisman's work. Very few people do.

"We all know the basics of combat. The three of us will work with her on the basics. While we are working with her, you can call in Khalid's handler Lulu. She would be the best teacher and you all know it." I say bluntly. I watch as both the Headmaster and Kai cringe.

Lulu came to school here about 50 years ago. During her talisman selection, they forced her to choose a jewel because that was all they brought out. Her magic rebelled against the foreign piece and destroyed it. Lulu is now a Verndari woman without a talisman. To say she is bitter is an understatement. Most females look forward to their talisman selection. They dream about it since they are kids; I'm sure she was no different. Without her talisman, she barely passed her trial. Lulu and all her mates were in the infirmary for a week before they were healed enough to leave. She promised to never step foot on this campus ever again.

"I doubt they would help. After what happened, they have kept their distance and have no desire to help me." The Headmaster says honestly. I know how hard those events were on him. He wasn't part of the Council back then and had no power to change their decisions. When they insisted that only jewels be brought out for the selection, the Headmaster was forced to follow their commands. He has held himself responsible for the events ever since it happened. It's why he took the Council post; to ensure he had all the power necessary to protect all of his students.

"You tell them about Ori, and they will come. They'll want to help her as much as they can. Lulu is overly sensitive. There is no way she'd say no." I confidently tell the Headmaster. She will hate every second she is here, but she will definitely come.

"Okay." The Headmaster sighs. I'll make the call. "You can start training her this afternoon in the gym." He tells me.

I nod my head and then leave before his mind changes. Time to get my team prepared for the next few months. I expect they'll all be happy to have something to do. They are getting restless and have been bouncing off the walls. We've never had downtime like this before; none of us know what to do with ourselves.

When I get back to our room, Gylfi and Dain are sitting on the couch facing the door, clearly waiting on me to get back. "You guys want something to do?" I ask.

"About damn time." Gylfi says with relief. Out of all of us, he's had the most issues with sitting around. I laugh slightly at him. I intentionally leave long pause trying to draw out their anticipation. "Well..." Dain adds.

"We start training Ori, Cedrick, Khalid, Barrett, and Orion starting this afternoon."

"Why us?" Dain asked, curiosity clear in his voice.

"She selected a whip for her talisman." I state, and the shock is palpable on both their faces. "They are going to call Lulu in to help, but we are going to start Ori's training until Lulu can get here. We know the basics. Besides, if she doesn't succeed at her trial, we will lose a brother. I will not let that happen."

24: ORI

A Girlfriend is just as Essential as your Mates

-Ljot

Cedrick's brothers suck. We have been training with them for a few hours and I feel like I'm dying. I love my new whip, but part of me wishes I picked a jewel like the other Verndari women do. While they get to sit in a classroom barely lifting a finger, I have been with the guys doing crazy crap like running the halls and stairwells, doing burpees, and lifting weights. Only crazy people do shit like this. Sweat is coating every inch of my skin. It sucks.

What makes the situation worse is that I have been able to hear everyone's thoughts for the past hour. It has been very distracting. Ryuu has a strange fascination with trying to kill us all. He likes it entirely too much. The only reason I'm willing to overlook it is due to the bond he has with his brothers. It is a physical connection that I could easily sense. Way stronger than what anyone probably realizes. He would do anything for anyone of them, which I respect. Gylfi and Dain understand this training as a necessary evil. They both felt pity for me about 15 minutes in. If I had the energy, I would punch them. I hate being pitied. Unfortunately, I don't have the energy. So they both get a pass today.

Currently, I am laying on the ground huffing and puffing, hoping that this nightmare would end. "You kill her already, Ryuu?" Asks a high-pitched voice. Another girl? I think, causing me to lift my head off the ground enough to get a look at her. She looks tall from this angle, but then again everyone does. I smile cause the first thing I notice about her is that she is wearing pants. A girl after my own heart. There is hope after all; I might find one female friend in this joint.

As she talks to Ryuu, I continue to analyze her. She has purple and black hair pulled into a tight bun on the back of her head. She is wearing a pair of tight black slacks and a black halter top that molds to her like a second skin. On her back is a long weapon. It looks like a double-bladed sword. The swords on either end of the staff appear to be long, thin daggers. Behind her are two similar looking men with black hair that falls to their shoulders. Their eyes are the same solid black, and both have prominent cheekbones. They look so similar that I immediately wonder if they are twins or at least biological brothers. They even have the same scowls on their faces telling me to stay out of their way. Noted.

"I didn't think I'd see the day when you would be back here, Lulu." Gylfi says from behind me.

"I couldn't let them send her to the wolves if I can help." She tells him right before she looks at me for the first time.

"You dead yet?" she asks with humor lacing her voice.

"Feels like it." I grumble dropping my head back to the ground groaning. Her high-pitched giggle echoes all around. "Don't hold it against Ryuu, he means well, I promise." She says with a smile as she reaches her hand out for me to take. Realizing I can no longer just lay here, I take her hand and stand up, groaning from the pain the simple motion causes. I didn't know it was possible to be this sore.

"I'm Lulu. I'm here to help you." She says genuinely.

"Ori." I respond even though I'm sure she probably already knows my name. Most people around here do.

"Why don't Ryuu and I give you a demonstration; that way you get a picture of what you are striving for." she suggests.

"Only if you kick his ass." I say needing some payback for all the bullshit he put me through the last few hours. This causes all the guys, aside from Ryuu, to chuckle. Ryuu just holds his heart like I have offended him. I doubt that man gets easily offended.

For the next ten minutes, I watch Lulu in awe. The blades on her double-bladed sword occasionally light up with purple. When she swings the sword at Ryuu, I can't take my eyes off it as electrical sparks fly up and down the staff making the sword pointed at him the primary hub of the electrical energy. At one-point Ryuu collapses without Lulu even touching him. The only sign he is in pain are his hands clutching both sides of his head. He manages to get up, which just seems to frustrate Lulu. The final blow comes when she uses the sword to take his legs out from under him. He drops to the floor with a loud thud and quickly puts a sparking purple blade up to his throat.

"I think you made your point, Lulu." Ryuu grunts from the ground.

"She did ask me to kick your ass." She says chuckling as she puts her weapon back on her back. The smirk on her face tells me just how much she enjoys showing the boys up.

Once she seems settled, she looks around at all nine boys and says, "Out."

"But..." my four men protest, not liking the thought of me being left alone.

"No buts." She says glaring at them. "You can wait outside the door. I'm sure there are important things that you haven't told her. She needs to know them sooner rather than later. And instead of waiting for you four to realize that you should have told her already. I'm going to. You guys can wait right outside the door." They sigh in defeat. It is crystal clear that she isn't going to change her mind. My men walk over, each giving me a kiss on my forehead before I watch them walk out with the other guys. The door shutting sounds louder as it reverberates through the room. Now it's just the two of us.

Lulu leads me over to the far side of the room. I lean my back on the wall and slide down to the ground. Sitting with my knees up, I wait patiently, not knowing where this conversation is going.

"I am sorry for everything you have gone through." Lulu says sympathy and understanding in her voice.

"What do you know?" I ask her.

"Only the basics and I suspect it is just the surface of reality. Just know that your men will be next to you for everything from this moment forward. They will do whatever they can to help you heal. I understand that healing is going to take time, but right now, time is not on your side. All the bullshit you have experience in the past you need to push down. At least for now. Once we get you out of here alive, you can take all the time in the world to heal." Hearing the possibility of my demise again shakes me to my core. I just don't understand why they are so careless about life.

"But there are so few females. Shouldn't they want to make sure that every Verndari female survives?" I question.

"Logically yes." She starts. "But the Council is afraid of females that choose weapons. Add to the fact that you can access all four focuses and I guarantee you they are terrified of you. The men on the Council don't like feeling inferior, and that is exactly what you make them feel. So... I'm here to help ensure that you get out of here. As soon as you pass the trial, they will no longer have the hold on you that they do now. The trial is only 2 months away, so we don't have much time. While the other two girls will only have a mental trial. You will have to prove both your mental strength as well as your physical. We are meant to be in their military, so the physical tests are quite gruesome. This is where they will try to kill you." Hide my death behind the veil of a failed test, why the hell not. I don't know much about them, but it sounds like something they'd do.

"So," she continues, "to ensure you are at your full power, you will train with Ryuu every afternoon. I will help you afterward learning how to utilize your weapon in both conventional and unconventional ways. Also, you need to have sex with all four of your men. Like yesterday." She bluntly tacks in on the end like we were talking about the weather.

"What?!" I say, unable to hide my shock. Apparently get to know them is overrated.

"Sex completes the bond and strengthens your magic. A solid bond allows you to focus and manipulate your magical energy more easily. With everything you have been through, they don't expect you to compete the bond prior to the trial. They will try to use that to their advantage." Her logic makes sense. But fuck, I didn't expect to have this type of conversation today.

"Okay." I say. What the fuck else was I supposed to say. I wasn't about to protest. Have you seen my men? The thought of having sex with them is very enticing. But is that what they want? Do they want that kind of relationship with the hot mess that is me?

25: UNKNOWN

Always watch out for those you'd least expect.

-Ljot

The tower I am in conceals me nicely. This section of the school has long been closed off. It used to house all our women, but as our numbers continued to decline, it was eventually shutdown; the hall is too much of a reminder of all the struggles our society has gone through.

This section of the school has no power, making it nice and dark. I am currently standing on one of the balconies that overlook the front of the school. From this vantage point, I can see anyone that comes and goes from the school. When I saw Lulu arrive, I had to stop myself from growling out my frustrations. I didn't anticipate her arrival. I'm not an idiot, I knew the Headmaster would attempt to call her in, but I didn't expect her to agree to come.

I thought I had given Lulu enough heartache during her time here that nothing would entice her to come back. It is unfortunate that I was wrong. Lulu is going to spill our secrets to Ori in the blink of an eye; Ori won't be as in the dark as I originally expected.

I'm going to have to up my game if I have any hope of getting rid of her. It will be more of a challenge; I love challenges.

"He is here, master," my servant says from behind me. My servant has been with me for the last one hundred and fifty years. He obeys me out of fear. Most Verndari would have a problem with that, but I wouldn't have it any other way. His fear ensures his loyalty. To make sure he never thinks about going against me, his family's safety is being held as collateral. If he ever goes against me, I will wipe them all out.

"Perfect timing." I tell him as I turn around to face him, and the man I summoned two days prior. He arrived in all black and is wearing a black cloak concealing his features. His attempts at concealing himself don't surprise me. Most people try to conceal themselves around me. What he doesn't realize is that I don't need to physically see him in order to know what he looks like. A gift of mine I have embraced since my 18th birthday.

"Did anyone see you arrive?" I ask, needing to be certain. Anyone seeing his arrival will ruin our chances. No need to make this more difficult than it already is.

"Did you see me arrive?" He asks with an attitude. If his skills weren't as good as they say, I would strike him down right where he stands. Instead, I just shake my head; I need him, at least for now. He should know better than to get on my bad side.

"Then no one saw me." He says with a cocky attitude that he should have left at home.

"Get rid of her." I tell him, deciding to get straight to the point.

"Who?" He asks. He knows who. News of our newcomer traveled through our race within a day. News of her potential power traveled to everyone within hours. We are a gossipy bunch. Usually it annoys me, but this time I have found it quite useful.

"You damn well know who." I say, no longer able to keep my irritation out of my voice.

"Why are you so scared of her? She is just one girl." He says attempting to get under my skin. Unfortunately for him, he succeeded.

"NO ONE SHOULD HAVE THAT KIND OF POWER. THAT POWER SHOULD HAVE BEEN MINE... MINE. BUT TO GIVE IT TO A GIRL. A GIRL THAT DOESN'T EVEN KNOW WHO SHE IS, IS AN OUTRAGE. IT'S MINE!" I scream right in his face.

"You might want to keep your voice down unless you want someone to know your here." The man says enjoying my brief outburst a little too much.

"Here." I say, handing him the large onyx jewel I promised. "You'll get the spell once she is no longer my problem. Don't fail." I turn dismissing him and look back out over the entrance to the school. The sounds of my servant and the man's footsteps lets me know they are on their way out. When the door finally thuds, I know they left. With any luck, by this time tomorrow Ori will no longer be my problem.

26: ORI

Love who you are.

-Ljot

I have been hiding out in the bathroom for the past half-hour. All four guys have knocked on the door and asked me if I'm okay. Physically I'm doing fine, better than I am used to being honestly. Mentally, I'm freaking out a bit. My time growing up has not been an easy one. I am certain that all four men at least suspect that, but they don't truly know everything I had to endure. I have dreamt of having someone for myself, but I didn't expect to find it for years. I knew I would need time to work through everything that my foster family put me through. Time that according to Lulu, I don't have.

Lulu has been in my position before, so I am forcing myself to trust her; she has given me no reason not to, but trust is hard for me. If I follow her advice, I will walk out of this room and jump all four of my men. As tempting as it is, I don't feel like I have it in me right now. I'm too damaged, both inside and out. Who wants someone that is as damaged as I am?

"I'm coming In." Cedrick suddenly says from the other side of the door. He easily pops the door open, even though it was locked. I guess locking the doors is a moot point. I watch him through the mirror as he walks up behind me and has worry in his eyes. He doesn't say anything until he is right behind me, holding me by my hips. I really like when the guys do that.

"What is going on in that beautiful head of yours?" He asks.

If only he knew. My mind keeps flipping between imagining what it would be like to be with them and seeing flashbacks of my past.

I'm standing in his study for the third time this week. The study has a distinctive smoky smell to it that never seems to go away. This place is his personal haven and my personal hell. He has my hands cuffed above my head with my bare back facing him. It didn't take long for me to realize that he got off on other people's pain. One time of being his personal whipping post was really all it took.

The scars from my last time encounter with him are just starting to heal. With the crack of his whip, I feel fresh pain radiating from my back. After a few more hits from the whip, I can feel the old wounds opening back up. My stubbornness is the only thing that is keeping me from screaming.

I don't hear the rest of my men rushing into the bathroom. I don't hear their shouts of worry. My mind isn't with them anymore. It is in the past; a past that has had a negative impact on the future I crave. It isn't until gentle hands grab ahold of both of my cheeks that I am brought back to reality. "You're not there anymore, Ori. Come back to us." Khalid says desperately.

"Did you see that?" I ask Khalid. Cedrick's hands on my hips tighten.

"Like I was there." He admits solemnly. "I would have given anything to make that experience disappear. I wanted so desperately to pull you away. When that didn't work, I would have settled on killing the bastard. Unfortunately, I can't kill a memory."

"That was 2 years ago, Khalid. The damage is much worse now. You aren't going to want someone like me. I'm too damaged."

"Oh Elskan ... That is where you are very wrong." Barrett says. The other three men nod in agreement. "While I didn't see what you went through, there is nothing that could stop me from wanting you."

"You haven't seen the damage, Barrett." I whisper. I refuse to look at him though. I don't want to risk seeing pity in his eyes.

"Then show us. Let us show you that it won't run us off. We aren't going anywhere, Ori." He says adamantly.

I don't know why I do it, but I find myself agreeing to Barrett's crazy plan. Why I agreed... I have no Idea. I don't even look at myself anymore, too repulsed by the damage that was left behind. Why they would want to see how destroyed my body is, I'll never understand. But in the end, I couldn't say no to him. That is how I end up lying face down on the bed in just my bra and panties. They left a few minutes ago, giving me some time on my own. I quickly stripped before my nerves got the better of me.

Deciding to just get the inevitable over with, I call my men mentally. I didn't know if it would work. I briefly smile when within 30 seconds of calling for them, the door opens. I guess it is a thing, I think, as I hear the door shut. The gasp of disbelief is the first thing I hear. Within seconds I burst into tears knowing that these men, the men that are supposed to be mine, will never want me.

27: BARRETT

Our Most Precious Treasures are the ones we Love

-Ljot

I heard her! I didn't think that would happen so soon. It's a wonderful development that I didn't expect. I looked over at all the other men and they must have heard her too because we all had big smiles on our faces. Khalid and Cedrick, who were both pacing the room not moments before, had stopped dead in their tracks and whipped their heads in my direction. Thank fuck we were not hallucinating.

We were still for 10 seconds max until the shock wears off before we all quickly head back to the bedroom. What I see when I enter shocks me. I couldn't stop the gasp that escaped me. Her back is covered in scars and welts that have healed wrong. There are more scars than healthy skin, which makes me want to kill the bastard that did this to her. What the hell did those humans do to her? I am so angry that I don't realize she started crying. The other guys take two seconds to glare at me before they bolt towards our girl. FUCK! I think. She is crying because of me. I can feel it.

Ori:

The tears keep falling and I just can't stop them. I have never cried so much in my life. But these men have quickly become the only people I have ever cared about. I don't want the scars of my past to scare my men away. I didn't realize until this moment how much I needed them.

I am taken aback by two gentle hands are turning my head. Barrett is kneeling at my level so that I can look him in the eyes. "I'm sorry for my reaction, Elskan. You are perfect just the way you are. I was just mad for you. I'd take it all away if I could. I'm not going anywhere. No one is going anywhere." He says right before he kisses me. The kiss is gentle, which is exactly what I needed in that moment. With tears still resting on my cheeks, he deepens the kiss. Seconds later, I feel three other mouths on my back. One is kissing the welts from my foster father's cigars. One is kissing up and down the never-ending scars from the whips that graced my back weekly for the past few years. And the last is kissing the scars my father made on the inside of my thighs in an attempt to keep me away from other men. When he made those, he said he wanted to ruin me. At first, I stayed strong and believed that the only way I was ruined is if I let him win. Eventually, enough scars were added that I believed him.

I go from crying because I genuinely believed that my men were going to run for the hills to feeling more loved than I ever really thought possible. When the mouth by my thighs suddenly kisses my pussy, I can't stop myself from moaning into Barrett's mouth. I feel a hand slide my panties aside just enough for a tongue to be able to enter me, I really want to grab ahold of whoever's head that is so that I can keep them there. Unfortunately, I am still on my stomach. My fingers start grasping at the sheets, itching to touch whoever is back there. Barrett chuckles at my lips, obviously enjoying my torture.

"Don't worry, Elskan, I've got you." He says. I watch him as he reaches down, and I suddenly feel a head pushed harder into my pussy. The tongue goes deeper, and my moans quickly get louder. I feel myself reaching for a destination that my body has never been to before. I feel like I am lingering on an edge, waiting in anticipation for something. When I feel a pinch to my clit, I convulse and screams quickly leave my mouth. I am sure others at the school can hear me, but in this moment, I don't give a fuck. "Good Elskan." Barrett whispers in my ear. "Now are you going to let me show you how much you mean to us?" He asks. "I'd love to be inside of you." He states in a husky tone that I have not heard from him. I whimper as his statement causes my pussy to contract again. An action that I didn't think was possible.

When the beautiful tongue finally slips out of me, Cedrick suddenly says, "I think her answer is a hell yes." He says bluntly. "at least that is what her pussy said," he continues as he slides my panties down my legs.

"Words Ori." Barrett suddenly demands of me.

"Yes." I whisper. The words are barely out of my mouth before I feel Barrett lift me up and flip me onto my back. In no time, I am laying lengthwise on the bed with my head dangling off. I take a second to look around and all my men are naked already. When the hell did that happen?

Barrett positions himself between my legs. At the same time, Khalid and Orion are kneeling on my sides, holding my hands down. I let my head fall down and Cedrick is at my head. His dick right at eye level.

"Sorry Elskan, this is going to hurt." Barrett suddenly says right before I feel his cock slam into me. He isn't gentle, but I don't need gentle. I feel him pull all the way out of me and then slam back in. I feel myself climbing faster than ever. The combination of the blood rushing to my head and his brutal assault of my pussy is the best feeling in the world.

I lose track of time until I finally break. I feel myself squeezing his dick, milking it, as hot spurts erupt inside of me. Seconds later, all my other men erupt all over my skin. I feel their seed land on my sides and my chest. I lay limp when I feel fingers rubbing the seed all around my skin. Then suddenly I feel fingers enter my pussy. I lift my head up, curious about what is going on. Khalid is smirking as I watch Cedrick and Orion follow Khalid's lead. Both of them scoop some of their seed off my skin and shove it deep into my pussy. "Ours." They all say simultaneously as if possessed. Fuck if that doesn't make me shiver in desire. What are these men doing to me?

28: KHALID

Surprise spices up life

-Ljot

W e all ended up sleeping in a pile after last night's escapades. If you would have asked me a week ago to sleep in the same bed as other men, I would have called you crazy. Last night I felt more at home in bed with Ori and the rest of the guys, than I have felt in a long time.

While part of me wanted to stay in bed like the rest of them, I forced myself to get up and go to the kitchen. I haven't cooked in a while and cooking calms me and helps me think. Surprised? Most people are. It's a hobby I took up after being forced out of the academy.

The kitchen in our room is basic, a small 2 burner stovetop, oven, and microwave. I wouldn't be able to make a large 5 course dinner in here, but breakfast will be no problem. I rummage around in the fridge, excited to find all the ingredients for eggs benedict. It is one of my favorite breakfast foods, and I rarely have a chance to cook it. I'm not going to turn down the chance now.

I decide to make some bacon to go with it. I mean, who doesn't like bacon? When I am taking the last piece of bacon off the grill, my girl comes in. Slowly, I might add. She is clearly not a morning person.

She ends up stopping just inside the door. Seconds later, her eyes light up. "Is that bacon? Please tell me that is bacon?" She asks, excitement entering her voice.

"It is bacon." I say with a smile on my face as I make my way towards her. When I get within a few inches of her she whispers, "Morning."

"Good Morning." I say as I pull her to me so that our chests are plastered together. My cock instantly swells. "That is all for you, sweetheart. How is my pussy doing this morning?" I ask none to quietly. The blush that covers her skin is beautiful.

"Wet... now." She admits grumbling into my chest.

"It's mine tonight." I tell her, making her even redder. I reluctantly pull away and grab her hand, pulling her to the kitchen bar where I already have a plate waiting for her.

Ori:

Breakfast was delicious. Out of all my men, I didn't expect Khalid to be the one that was able to cook. I have never had an eggs benedict before, but it quickly became my new favorite breakfast. He can cook for me any time he likes.

After Khalid's declaration this morning, the deliciousness of the food was the only thing that kept me from saying fuck breakfast. His one statement made me wet and horny. If his cooking sucked, I would have probably jumped him instead of eating. Now there is no time to fit a quickie in before class. What the hell have these men done to me?

Today we end up in the same room we started in yesterday. I was relieved to see that we were the only ones in there. I wasn't in the mood to deal with the other girls today. After only five minutes of waiting, our instructor arrives. I was expecting Master Kai, but Lulu and her men are the ones that walk in. I smile. I like Lulu. Somehow, I know that she only wants the best for me. Other than my men, she is the only other individual I trust in this place.

"Who was it?" She suddenly asks with a smile on her face.

Confusion must be clear on my face because she just laughs and looks at my men.

"It was me." Barrett says blushing. Why is he blushing? I question before it slowly dawns on me what she is asking. I can feel the heat going straight to my face; I must be as red as a tomato.

"There is nothing to be embarrassed about Ori. If I didn't have to know, I wouldn't have asked. Now that you have mated with Barrett, you should be able to access his powers. Take out your whip." She instructs.

I take it from my hip and allow it to unwind until the end is resting on the floor. She directs all the men to stand around me in a circle. Her men join them leaving the two of us in the center.

"When your talisman is a weapon, you can combine your magic with the weapon. There are numerous possibilities on how you do that. The options are as vast as your imagination. Now... time to figure out one option. Isn't this exciting?" I think she is more excited than I am.

"Barrett, can you explain your powers?" Lulu asks him.

I close my eyes as I listen to Barrett as he explains his primary powers; he can implant memories or take them away. I am in awe of him. Never in my wildest dreams did I ever imagine I would be capable of something like that.

Lulu's directions are simple; think of an image and put it in someone's head. "Keep it simple." She explains. "It can be as simple as a tulip or raindrop. The more detail in the image, the more magic it takes to implant. Start with something simple or something that you know really well." Sounds easy, right?

I look at Cedrick and imagine the beautiful sunrise I used to watch every morning. I have seen it every day for two years, so it should be easy to imagine and implant, right? As the memory comes to mind, my whip glows a beautiful, bright red.

"Anything?". Lulu asks everyone.

Everyone shakes their heads, making me feel instantly defeated. Then out of instinct I use my whip and direct it right at Cedrick. I don't hit him, but when I hear the crack in the air, I push the memory in his direction. The smile on his face is all I needed. He sees it.

"It's beautiful." He says.

"I did it!" I say practically jumping up and down.

"Good job! Now give the memory to everyone else." I assumed that task would be easy. It was easy for my guys, but when I tried to give it to her men, it was a lot harder. The whip had to be a lot closer to them for it to work. I was sweating and about ready to collapse by the time I was done.

"Good. Now to figure out how to remove it." Lulu said. I groan. I thought I liked that woman. Now I am thinking she is just as bad as Ryuu.

29: ORI

Your Past Experiences Shape who you are

-Ljot

For hours I stood in the middle of the circle, trying to remove the simple memory that I had given everyone. Everything I tried failed. It wasn't until the whip contacted Khalid's arm that I was successful. I didn't realize it at the time though because I am in the middle of having a panic attack. The sound of the whip hitting his flesh caused my brain to go back to a time when I had felt it on my own skin.

"No one is going to want you" he says yet again as the whip hits my back, breaking my flesh. I can feel the blood starting to slip down my back, gravity pulling at it. "Who wants someone as damaged as you? No one. I am going to destroy you for anyone else." He sneers and the whip whistles through the air and hits my thighs.

"You are not him, Ori." Orion says from somewhere far away. "You could never be him." He continues. "Khalid is fine." He says trying to reassure me.

"I am fine, Love. You didn't hurt me." Khalid says in a soothing voice.

I blink my eyes, trying to dislodge the memory and bring into focus the men standing in front of me. All four of my men are in front of me with worry in their eyes. "Are you sure?" I whisper, needing to hear it again.

"Positive. The beautiful sunrise you gave me is gone though." He says smiling. His concern is immediately replaced with pride. No one has ever been proud of me before. I just wish his pride would help me cope with my reality. I'm not sure it's going to be enough.

"I HAVE TO HIT PEOPLE WITH MY WHIP TO TAKE MEMORIES AWAY?" I question screaming. "I can't do that." I push through them and start to pace the floor. I can feel everyone watching me. Lulu and her men think I am breaking. I can sense it in their emotions. I've never broken before and I don't want to start now. But I can't hurt others like what was done to me, even for just a single moment. "I'm not sure I can do that. Put people through what I've been through." I finally say whispering. My hesitancy to do what needs to be done makes me feel weak. I hate feeling weak, but this is one thing I am not sure I am capable of.

"I've seen everything you have gone through." Orion finally admits to me. Why didn't he tell me sooner? "We'd never expect you to do those things. This is different. A whip doesn't have to cause that much violence. You can make contact without hurting anyone." Orion says

My head falls when I realize how much he knows about me. I can't help but question what the others know. Am I ready for them to know how bad my life really was?

"I haven't seen the extent of your memories like Orion has, but I know that you will never be like the people that hurt you. Your whip is a tool, nothing more." Cedrick says, trying to reassure me.

"I can't see memories like they can. I would be lying to you if I said I didn't want to know what you went through. I desperately want to know, but I am waiting for you to tell me on your own time." Barrett admits.

"Thanks." I whisper unsure of what else to say. Taking a deep breath, I ask, "What do I do?" I trust my men with all my heart.

Orion:

Lulu and her men quickly disappeared to the far side of the room when they realized that Ori was having a panic attack. They are gathered in a circle, whispering to each other. All of us appreciated the space; I doubt Ori would want everyone to know how bad her life really was. If any of Lulu's mates saw the memory that Ori was experiencing, they aren't saying anything. I don't even have to ask to know they would willingly join us to kill the bastard.

I know Barrett and Khalid have their suspicions, but they don't really know the extent of her experiences. It is far worse than what they could ever imagine. Cedrick has seen more than them, but even he doesn't have the full picture.

It takes us a moment to pull her out of her panic. She puts on a brave face and says she is willing to learn, but even I can sense how difficult it is going to be for her. To properly learn how to use her whip in a short period of time is going to be a battle of wills. She is going to struggle, but I have faith she will conquer her fears. She is the strongest woman I know.

For the last part of the day, we all watch as Lulu attempts to teach her how to manipulate her whip. She is working with a dummy and every time it hits too hard you see her flinch. We all fear she will fall back into another flashback. The four of us are on edge, ready to pull her out of her past at a moment's notice. Pride swells through us as we watch her work through her fear. Ori pauses after each impact re-centering her mind. Each pause is excruciating to watch. But luckily, as time moves on, that pause gets shorter and shorter.

With ten minutes left, I know what Lulu is going to suggest. "Time to try it on a person." Khalid immediately walks toward our girl. He needs Ori to know he trusts her. She needs to know she won't hurt him. They both need this right now.

"I trust you." He tells her while holding her face in his hands. The whole encounter only last seconds before he lets go and moves to stand about 6 feet in front of her.

We all watch as Ori battles with herself. The mental battle is hard to watch, but I suspect it is even harder to feel. Barrett is frowning and wincing. His new connection to her makes it so he can easily feel her. I am sure he senses everything that she is feeling. Based on the look on his face, he doesn't like it one bit.

It takes about five minutes, but eventually our girl attempts to pull a memory out. We watch as the whip gracefully wraps around Khalid's upper calf. He doesn't flinch; he just stands there watching our girl. Showing his complete faith and trust in her.

Ori:

I don't know why Khalid volunteered. I already took my memory away from him, so what would I take. I am panicking inside. What if I take away the wrong memory? What if the memory is something he wants to remember, and I can't put it back? When I finally just go for it, the moment my whip wraps around his leg, flashes of his memories float through my head. When I find one of him slipping in a puddle of mud, something I know I wouldn't mind forgetting about, I pull at it trying to bring it towards me.

I watch in fascination as the magic in the whip glows brighter and forms into a small ball at the tip of my whip. Slowly, the bright spot travels up the whip towards me until it absorbs into my skin. Once the last of the red magical light is gone, the whip's magic dissipates until it has completely dimmed.

I look up and multiple people have their jaws dropped.

"Well, I have seen nothing like that before," Lulu says, surprised. "Tomorrow we will have to work on speeding up the process." She continues smiling as if that idea is the best idea in the world.

"What did you take?" Khalid finally asks.

"You were slipping in a puddle." I say, hoping he won't be mad.

"You can keep it, love." He says as he grabs my hand and pulls me out of the door.

30: ORI

Magical Drain is Exhausting... Know your Limits.

-Ljot

By the time I finally make it back to our room, I am exhausted both mentally and physically. Learning to use Barrett's powers is more taxing than I ever thought possible. While I know a little about the Verndari focus's, my knowledge is limited. Orion planned on teaching me more, but there hasn't been any time. Out of the four focuses, mind, heart, gut instinct, and soul, Barrett's focus is the mind. As I felt my powers starting to drain, pressure built in my head. By the time we left Lulu I had a full-on migraine. Lucky for me, as time passed it slowly dissipated. *I'm going to have to ask Barrett about that in the morning,* I think, as I head straight for the dresser.

Wanting nothing more than to take a nice long nap in the comfiest cloths I can find, I open a dresser drawer searching for the sacred treasures so I can crash on the cloud bed that I have quickly come to love. I open the drawer an inch when time suddenly slows. I feel myself being pulled away by one of my men. Seconds later, we're forcefully pushed away by an unexpected blast. The seconds when I am flying through the air last a lifetime. Fuck, what was that?

I land on someone with a thud. I quickly compose myself and turn slightly to see that I have landed on Cedrick. His eyes are closed, making him look peaceful, but panic quickly rises inside of me. My hand goes to his chest, needing to know that he is safe. When I don't feel it rising and falling, I scream.

"CEDRICK!"

My breathing comes faster, and I start hyperventilating. Strong arms try to pull me off Cedrick, only making my screams intensify. I claw at the hands, unwilling to leave Cedrick. I can hear my heartbeat in my ears, drowning out everything else around me.

"I've got you love." Khalid says quietly, unphased by the damage I have done to his hands. Within seconds of hearing his soothing voice, the fight in me disappears. I turn and breakdown in his arms instead.

Cedrick:

I learned from a young age to trust my instincts. I didn't always understand why I needed to act a certain way, but I learned young never to ignore them.

Growing up, my house was located between the Verndari civilization and the human settlement. No one else lived there, just my strange family. As a child, I didn't understand why I differed from humans. They looked like I did, so I assumed we were the same. So, when I was bored and my parents were busy, I would sneak off to the park that all the human kids played in.

On the far side of the park, large rocks were stacked on top of each other giving the children a place to climb. King of the Mountain was a common game I would play with the other kids. Next it was a field that was more dirt than grass. It our go to place for tag. Sometimes one of the children would bring a ball and we would play a game of soccer. That day we were just goofing off on the stone structure. About an hour into being at the park, my instincts told me to keep one of the kids at the park. I ignored my instincts and watched as he left. Seconds later, I watch as my father's car runs right over the boy I was just playing with as if he didn't care that he took a life.

That memory has haunted me since the day it has happened. I have lost track of how many times it has played over and over in my head. I regret not listening to my instincts that day and I learned to always follow them. They weren't wrong then, and they have never been wrong since.

So, when instinct tells me to pull her back, I do just that. I don't question it. Seconds later we are both blown backwards by an explosive force to the other side of the room. She lands on top of me with a thud. I feel my head hit the hard cement floor and seconds later everything goes black.

Shouts surrounding me brings me closer to consciousness. At first, I can't tell who the shouting is directed at. Most of the guys are swearing. Why?

It takes a few moments for my consciousness to come back enough to realize how bad our situation really is. Lifting my head slightly, I see the dresser blown to shreds. Wood chips are everywhere, and the corner of the bed closest to the dresser is broken off and dangling in a 6-foot hole in the floor. If I hadn't pulled Ori away, she would have died.

It is in that moment that I realize her weight is no longer on top of me. I start panicking, wondering if I didn't pull her away fast enough. I sigh in relief when I see that Ori is in Khalid's arms. Her face is plastered to his chest and you can see the tears falling down her cheeks. The outlines of some cuts and bruises are showing on her arms. Other than those cuts and bruises, she seems to be intact.

"He is fine." Khalid says, trying to reassure her. His face and voice are both soft, but his eyes only reflect anger. Whoever did this is going to pay. I start laughing, unable to stop myself; I'd hate to be that guy.

Ori:

Cedrick's laughter has my head whipping in that direction. Relief at him being okay has the tears flowing even harder. I can't lose him already; I just found him.

"You won't lose him." Barrett says from the other side of the massive hole in our bedroom.

I glare at him. The fact that he knows what I'm thinking is going to take some getting used to. What would he say if I thought of other men?

"Don't you dare." He says practically growling at me. I just laugh. "Don't answer all the questions I have in my head then." I say with a smirk, trying to tease him.

"Come on, love" Khalid says as he guides me out of the room.

"But Cedrick?" I question. I need to know he is okay.

"Go with Khalid, sweetheart. I promise I am fine, but you can check me out later if it would make you feel any better." He says winking at me as he stands up.

"If you're sure." I say, letting Khalid lead the way.

As we leave, the Headmaster and Master Kai pass by. They both have a frown on their faces. I watch them head straight for my other men. The five of them are in a circle, talking in a whisper. The seriousness of the situation is plastered all over their faces.

We are almost out of the apartment when Cedrick comes racing up to us. Shouldn't he be moving slower under the circumstances? I mentally question as he is speaking with Khalid. I come back to the conversation as Khalid nods his head and backs up slightly to give Cedrick and I some space.

"You are really okay?" I immediately ask him, needing reassured again.

"It's going to take a lot more than that to get rid of me." He says. "I'm glad you're okay. That could have killed you.". He says seriously.

"I'm okay because of you." I say starting to tear up again.

"I have always trusted my instincts. Following them is part of who I am. I learned the hard way that not following them has disastrous consequences. My instincts are the only reason I could save you. I am asking you to trust my instincts as much as I do."

"I trust you, Cedrick." I say meaning every word.

"Good… you need to fuck Khalid." He says bluntly.

I can't help it, my jaw drops. That is the last thing that I expected him to say. After a brief delay, I just start laughing. What the hell else am I supposed to do?

"You can use our room." Ryuu says as he and his team enter our apartment. He tosses the keys to me, which I easily catch. His serious look has my laughter stopping.

"I would do what he says." Ryuu continues, "Not following Cedrick's instincts is never a good idea."

"Come on, Love." Khalid says, taking the keys from my shaking hands and leading us next door. The walk was a quiet one. The door to their room was only a few hundred yards down the hallway. For the entire walk, the only question in my mind was, what the fuck has this day turned into?

31: GYLFI

Betrayal is Painful

-Ljot

We've been at the school for approximately a week and to be honest, the other guys have been enjoying their relaxation time. Other than the few occasions we were helping to train Ori, they have either been here reading, playing practical jokes on each other, or in the rec room stealing the pool tables. I play along, needing them to continue to see me as family, but this trip put a kink in my plans. It isn't anything I can't manage; I just have to be strategic. I am surprised I have found enough alone time to still get my job done.

    Right now, we are all gathered in the living room making plans for Ori's training tomorrow, when we feel it. The blast makes our room shake. We don't have to ask what it is. As part of Ryuu's team, we have all seen enough to know exactly what it is without having to ask. A bomb went off. The aftershocks tell me it came from the direction of Cedrick's room. I watch all my brother's eyes as the realization hits them at the same time. As their eyes grow wide, they are out of their chairs and out the door before I can blink. I shouldn't have expected anything less. Cedrick is "family" after all.

I follow quickly behind them and see Cedrick talking to Ori. From what I can see she has a few cuts and bruises, but that is all. I would've thought she would have had more severe injuries.

"You can use our place." Ryuu says from ahead of me as he throws the keys to Ori. Use our place for what? I internally question as I curse myself for not paying more attention to my teammates. I shouldn't have allowed myself to lag even seconds behind them. Now, I am missing vital information that I know will kick me in the ass later.

She catches the keys like a natural, but her jaw drops, not expecting that kind of reaction from Ryuu. I watch as Khalid comes back to her side and grabs her hand as Ryuu tells Ori not to ignore Cedrick's instincts. Cedrick's instincts are always right; they have helped a lot of Verndari and saved our own skins more than once. Most of our kind underestimate people like him. They are fools if you ask me.

When we hear the door close with a soft click, we go to their bedroom which is undoubtedly the epicenter of the blast. We barely get in the door when all three of us stop in our tracks. It has been a while since we have seen this kind of damage.

"FUCK" Ryuu says from ahead of us. He is glaring at the hole in the floor and the half-demolished bed dangling down into the room below. The wall with the dresser has scorch marks traveling all the way up to the ceiling. I can't help but smirk. I love this shit.

"Take that smile off your face." Ryuu demands as he faces me. "Just because you're a bomb expert doesn't mean that you get to appreciate the work that could have killed your bother." He's angry. "This should have killed him; he is lucky to be alive." He reiterates. He is extremely lucky to be alive; I guarantee that the only thing that saved them was his damn instincts. No one remembers to plan for those.

"Well… it didn't." I say bluntly. "And I always appreciate another's work. You're aware of that, so why would this be any different."

"This could have killed your brother and his mate. That is why this is different. Have some fucking respect" I don't respond, instead, I just watch as he storms over to Ori's other three mates. They are angry and wanting revenge. Even I can't blame them?

Ryuu:

Leaving Gylfi to his thoughts, I head over to Cedrick and his new partners. They are all standing on the far side of the hole, staring at the destruction. I take a second to look them over and other than the fact that they all look pissed, and rightfully so, they only appear to have a few scrapes and bruises on them. Cedrick has a little more than the others, but I suspect he was closer to the blast than Barrett and Orion. All in all, the damage could've been much worse.

"How the hell did someone get this close to her?" Cedrick immediately asks, fuming. His fists are clutched together at his side and are quickly turning white. A white shimmery haze of his power is radiating off him, telling us just how close he is to losing it.

"We'll figure it out." I tell him as Dain and Gylfi finally join the group. "First things first, we need to find remnants of the bomb. It's the only way to get a clue about who did this." I remind him, hoping he will switch to work mode. "Dain and Gylfi, go to the floor below and see if you can find anything down there. Cedrick and I will look up here." I immediately instruct.

"What about us?" Barrett asks as Dain and Gylfi leave to follow my orders. "We aren't going to just sit around. Someone just tried to kill our mate." Demanding little fucker, isn't he? I have to hold a chuckle in; I am going to like them.

"I wouldn't expect you to sit out. I am not an idiot. You can help Cedrick and me but be sure to listen. You don't want to fuck this up for your mate." I say seriously, hoping they understand how important completing the job within the lines is for Ori. The Council will use any minor slip up to throw the investigation out. We can't allow that to happen.

Gylfi:

It doesn't take us long to make our way downstairs. The area that now has a vast hole in the ceiling is the very public lounge area… so, of course, there is an immense crowd. The ceiling is laying in pieces on top of one of the pool tables that Ryuu and Dain frequently steal from the students. Concrete powder from the floor above is scattered throughout the entire room. The televisions are cracked and useless. The chairs closest to the hole are all blown over. The crowd that is gathered obviously has new additions. Individuals covered in grey dust were present at the time of the explosion. Those students that are oddly clean had to come in afterward; probably to investigate the noise.

"Do not tell me you idiots touched something." Dain screams into the crowd, making all the noise and chatter stop instantly. The only sound you hear is the sound of items dropping to the floor. Idiots. I think as I hear them finally scatter, leaving us in peace to do our job.

We have done this sort of thing often enough to work cohesively without saying a word; the silence is peaceful. Slowly, we work our way around the room. Lifting up pieces of ceiling, moving the furniture, and digging inside piles of rubbish in an attempt to find the evidence we need. About an hour later, I hear Dain from the other side of the room.

"Found It!" He says, lifting a small red gem up. The color has completely faded, letting us know its power died with the explosion. "You know what this means, right?" he asks me.

"Yeah, Ryuu isn't going to like this development."

"Ryuu's anger will be nothing compared to her mates." He chides.

"What do you mean?" I ask, not understanding where he is going with this. I know he has seen Ryuu pissed off. Who could possibly be madder than him?

"You haven't seen pissed off mates before, have you?" Dain says.

"No." I grudgingly admit.

"Oh... you are in for a treat." He says with a smirk on his face.

Dain:

I rush up the stairs two at a time, trying to quickly get back to the other guys. I see them all digging through the debris, chucking the useless remnants to the only clean corner of the room; at least it was clean when I left.

"Found something." I announce, getting all their attention. I hold up the used gem and a round of fucks from both Cedrick and Ryuu tell me they know exactly what this means.

"What's that?" Barrett and Orion ask simultaneously.

I look at Ryuu, wondering how much information I can tell them. He just nods his head. A signature move of his giving me the okay. He trusts them. Under the circumstances, I can understand why.

"We have been chasing a bomber for the past twenty years. This gem is his signature. He is the only one that has ever eluded us. I would be surprised if this belonged to someone else, but I am going to have to analyze and compare it to the others to know for sure." I tell them.

"Go" Ryuu directs. Our brother's mate is at risk here. There are no limits to what we'll do to protect our family. That is what she is now... family.

"Cedrick, you guys can't do anything else, go spend time with your girl. She is going to need all four of you." Ryuu says.

"Come get us Dain as soon as you have information on that gem. I don't give a fuck what time it is." He demands. My eyebrows raise up slightly, I have never heard Cedrick be so demanding. Ryuu though doesn't look surprised.

"Of course, Cedrick," Ryuu says. "We wouldn't even think about excluding you. Now Go!" We watch as Cedrick, Barrett, and Orion all leave, no doubt doing exactly what Ryuu suggested.

"Since they are using our room, where are we going to go?" I ask, causing them to burst out laughing.

32: ORI

The Love of Each Mate is Precious and Unique

-Ljot

I don't know what I expected when we walked into Ryuu's room, but it wasn't what I found. Part of me expected the room to be a mess. I mean, three guys live here, but it was in pristine condition. I couldn't help but wonder which of the guys cleaned it every day. Someone had too; there wasn't a dust bunny in sight.

Just glancing around, I could tell the place was set up identically to the one I was in. The only difference was that the bedroom was off to the left instead of the right.

Khalid doesn't give me much time to look around as he quickly guides me through the main rooms, into Ryuu's bedroom, and straight to the bathroom. Their bathroom is decorated in calming blue and white colors. It contains a giant shower that could easily fit 6 people. The tiled shower differs from ours, with three shower heads and an entrance to the shower that's open so anyone would see you if they walked into the bathroom. There is a small inset cabinet on the far side of the room that no doubt holds towels. Across from the shower are two sinks with toothbrushes, toothpaste, and shaving supplies scattered about; the only indication that men live here.

Khalid let go of my hand just long enough to start all three shower heads. "Come here, sweetheart." he says urging me forward. I willingly walk towards him and as soon as I am within reaching distance, he strips me of my clothes.

"Let me take care of you." He says as he lifts my shirt over my head. I nod my head, liking the thought of someone taking care of me for once. It's a strange feeling for me, but one that I'm quickly learning to love.

I shiver when he gets me down to my bra and panties. He watches me with a glint in his eye for a brief moment before he slides his hands under the edges of my panties and slides them down my legs. I reach behind my back and help him out by unclasping my bra and letting it fall to the ground.

By now steam is gathering in the bathroom, letting us know that the water has warmed up. It doesn't take long for him to strip, allowing me a great view. I instinctually wet my lips with my tongue at the sight and Khalid groans in response.

"I'm going to get you cleaned up first" he says as he ushers me into the shower. The hot water hitting my skin feels like heaven. He gently turns me so that my back is facing him. His hands massage my scalp and I moan. I can't help it; it feels so damn good. I feel his dick get harder against my back.

When he turns me around, the look of lust in his eyes is intoxicating. He gently lifts my chin, allowing my head to hit the water. It isn't until my eyes close that I feel his hands wondering.

The smell of roses assaulting my nose is the only warning I get before I feel him rubbing soap on my skin. I am enjoying the feel of him touching me enough that I don't realize how long we stay in the shower. Every touch on my arms and caress on my legs makes me feel loved. When he finally starts massaging my breasts and touching the outside of my pussy, I melt. I hold back for as long as I can, but eventually I cave and find myself jumping him, allowing my legs to wrap around his waist. His hands hold on to my ass and his lips quickly descend onto mine.

I don't even notice our trek out of the bathroom until my back hits a wall. I can feel his desperation for me through his frantic kisses. His lips move down my chin and onto my neck. I feel my hips move against his abs in search for what it wants. I feel him chuckle against my neck as I hear the door open and my other three guys walk in.

As if he had it planned, Khalid slams his dick into me as the others watch on. "Don't close your eyes, sweetheart. I want you to keep your eyes on them the entire time." He whispers into my ear as he continues slamming into me. "Make sure you let them know how much you are enjoying this" He demands.

The words are no sooner out of his mouth when loud moans escape mine. I keep my eyes open and watch my men as they all slip their pants down just far enough for their dicks to pop free. All three of them start masturbating as I watch them. Barrett moves his hand slow and steady, like he is trying to savor this moment. Orion's moments are fast, like he can't help how much watching me affects him. Cedrick's moves his hand in a fast then slow pattern as he approaches us. At first, I think he is just trying to get a better view, but that quickly changes when he leans down and puts his lips on my nipple.

My entire pussy contracts around Khalid's dick as soon as Cedrick's lips make contact. I explode, pulling Khalid's seed from him like my body is craving it.

When I come down from my high, I collapse against Khalid's chest. I take in his scent and sigh when Cedrick's musty scent mixes with Khalid's minty aroma. I find my eyes closing of their own accord and fall asleep still in Khalid's arms.

33: UNKNOWN

Craving Power is a Dangerous Game

-Ljot

Gathered around all the Council members, I had to hide my pleasure when I heard the bomb go off. I was surrounded by too many people. Most of them worried about our new Verndari; too caught up with tradition to do what really needs to be done.

"Please tell me she made it?" One of the councilman worriedly asks.

"We better not have lost another one already."

"What will happen to her guys?" Someone else questions, assuming she didn't make it.

"I thought our security would have stopped a bomb from making it onto campus. How the hell did it get on campus?" the Headmaster asks.

How indeed.

All questions are quickly answered when moments later news spreads, letting us know that she had somehow survived. How the fuck did she survive? Hearing of her survival killed my excitement. I excused myself from the room, blaming my departure on a previous engagement. No one thought twice.

I have been waiting at our meet up spot since then. He knows he needs to meet up with me. I am not a patient man, so to be left here waiting for thirty minutes really grates my nerves. This man is really testing my patience.

When I finally hear the door open behind me, I immediately question what took him so long, making the venom obvious in my tone. If he didn't realize his mistake before, he does now.

"It's not that easy to get away. I can't look suspicious." He says making excuses for his late arrival.

"Don't leave me waiting again." I command; he should be grateful I am giving him a second chance. "Why is the girl still alive?"

"Cedrick's instincts." He says from behind me. Like that response should be sufficient. Instinctual Verndari are a laugh. Weaklings every last one of them.

"I don't give a fuck about his instincts. The girl should be dead."

The man I employed to kill the girl just starts laughing. I spin around and glare at him. No one laughs at me. My anger gets the better of me and I allow my magic to lift him off the ground and push him to the wall behind him. His laughing immediately stops, but a smirk is still on his face. I glare at him as I approach. He needs to know how angry this has made me; people know not to piss me off. To be honest, he is lucky to be alive; people have died for less.

"You haven't done your research on him, have you?" He questions. Why would I do research on some lowly spies? They're the individuals our kind use for dirty work and look down at. They couldn't possibly have any powers that would be a risk to me.

"If you had," he continues, "you would know that his instincts are never wrong. They are the strongest of any instinctual Verndari. Most people on the Council are afraid of them. Why do you think they put him in such a risky job?"

"None of that matters." I say seriously. "It's your job to anticipate them and make sure they don't get in the way of completing your job; kill the girl." I reiterate.

"You cannot anticipate his instincts. Plenty of people have tried and they have all failed."

"Then you need to be the first. I am sure you don't want your peers to learn about your extracurricular activities ... do you?" I threaten him. I stare at him, watching as sweat forms on his brow. He is finally nervous. "Make sure she dies." I reiterate as I finally allow my magic to drop him with a thud.

I hear him scurrying to leave as I turn around and head back towards the window that overlooks the campus. There are hundreds of our kind down below. You can see them in groups, frantically talking. You can tell which ones where in the area below the explosion. They all have debris in their hair, some even have black dust coating their skin.

They must have been the closest. The fact that they are now in groups gossiping doesn't surprise me in the slightest. These men can be just as bad as woman some days. I am sure the gossip isn't going to die down anytime soon. FUCK... between the gossip and the added security, my underlings job just got harder. All he had to do was kill her the first time. How fucking hard was that to do? Clearly harder than he thought. Maybe I should have just handled it myself.

34: ORI

I feel most at Home when I am with All my Men.

-Ljot

I wake up tucked between all four of my men. My head is still laying on Khalid's chest. I listen to his heartbeat and the soft breathing of my other men. It is soothing to listen too; makes me forget about everything that I have gone through. The near-death experiences don't matter when I am this peaceful. I lift my head to look out the window and see that it is my favorite time of day, sunrise. Regardless of where I was, sunrise was always my favorite time of day. It's no different here. Today's sunrise is filled with purples and yellows. Beautiful white fluffy clouds dot the sky. I smile, imprinting the image into my head alongside all the other sunrises I have witnessed in my life.

I carefully twist around and see Cedrick on the far side of the bed with my whip gripped tightly in his hand. He remembered... I think as I look at how peaceful he looks in his sleep.

"Are you going to quit staring at me?" Cedrick says with his eyes still closed, but a chuckle forming on his lips.

"Maybe" I answer as I scrunch my nose up, unhappy about being caught in my morning perusal. He opens one eye to look at me and chuckles when he sees my expression.

A long bang from the other side of the room has all my guys quickly bolting upright in bed and pushing me behind them. All four of my men are standing naked as the day they were born, guarding me from the unexpected intruder.

"Damn it Ryuu." Cedrick yells causing me to peak around my men. Ryuu is chuckling, loving this a little too much.

"Are you guys going to cover up?" He asks, never closing his eyes.

"It's your fucking fault for barging in on us." Cedrick grumbles. "If you didn't want to see anything, you should've knocked." He continues bluntly. "Why are you here anyway?" Cedrick asks, finally turning towards me and handing me my whip.

"Extra security. We leave in ten minutes for the cafeteria." He says.

"Why the cafeteria?" I ask, finally speaking up from behind my men.

"We need people to see you with their own eyes. Gossip has been running rampant all night. Some say you have lost an arm and have scars over most of your body. Some say you died, and your men are not far behind you. Some say you are in a coma in the hospital and they don't know when you will wake up. The gossip is not helping and in order for it to stop, they will have to see you themselves."

"How the hell did they come up with all that?" I ask, bewildered. Although the first one isn't entirely untrue.

All seven men are now laughing. "We'll meet you in the living room." Ryuu says never answering my question. I watch as he leaves, giving us space to get ready for the day ahead.

Ten minutes later, all eight of us are heading down the many hallways towards the cafeteria. As we approach, I hear the constant chatter from the other students, but the moment we open the doors, the entire room goes silent with the only sound being the clicking of silverware on dishes as they unexpectedly fall from the student's hands. The room itself is massive, with long picnic tables scattered about in various sizes. The ceiling is made up of multiple large glass windows allowing sunlight to shine throughout the room. On the far side is a buffet with food of all kinds for the taking.

As we walk straight for the buffet, ignoring all the awkward stares, I mumble, "This isn't awkward at all." My guys stick close to me the whole time. It's a comfort to have them close as all eyes are on me. I am so tense from being watched that I don't pay the least bit of attention to what I get for breakfast. Luckily, I am not a picky eater.

It isn't until all of us have gotten food that we head to a table at the far side of the room. The end of the table had plenty of space for all eight of us. While I was originally cringing at the thought of coming here, I end up really enjoying myself. I learned a lot about Ryuu and his men. He was happy to give me insight into some hilarious stories that involved Cedrick. I expected Cedrick to halt the stories, but he laughed along with the guys and even started stories that most people would have been embarrassed to share. It made me love him a little more.

After breakfast, we follow Ryuu. I expect him to lead us to the training room to work more with Lulu today. When we head outside and stop at a ropes course, I know immediately that my morning isn't going to involve Lulu. It's another Ryuu day which just makes me groan. He enjoys trying to kill me.

My entire morning involves me repeatedly going through the course. Every time I fell, Ryuu made me start over. My biggest problem was climbing up the rope; that shit is harder than it looks. I end up sliding back down the rope and landed on my ass more times than I care to admit. My hands are covered in rope burns.

Despite my failed attempts, Ryuu, the drill sergeant, makes me go through it alone over and over until I can finish it. I lost track of how many times I had to restart. By the time I finally finish it, I am sweating and quickly collapse on the ground. To be honest, I am surprised I am still conscious.

"Now, do it again with your guys." He directs.

"That is going to have to wait." Lulu says from behind him.

"Thank God." I say too loudly, causing Lulu to laugh. I like Lulu and even though she can be just as much of a hard ass as Ryuu, she is a little nicer about it... most of the time.

Lulu guides us to a field south of the ropes course. It is open enough that we have plenty of room to work with my whip. At first, we focus on learning basic magic that doesn't involve me touching my whip. She starts with levitation and learning to move things around. She directs me to move sticks around. With every attempt I make, my whip glows at my side. About an hour in, I can consistently move sticks from one side of the field to the other without breaking a sweat. The looks of approval on my men's faces make my heart sing.

"You are a quick study." Lulu says to me. "Now, take your whip and make the stick a weapon." She directs as Ryuu moves a target to the far side of the field.

I take a deep breath before finally taking my whip from my side. It quickly unravels down my side, but I can tell immediately that something is wrong. My hand tingles, and I can feel myself swaying on my feet. I feel a strange sensation flow through my body. It's not painful exactly; more paralyzing. When my feet give out from underneath me, I see my men running towards me as I collapse on the field as the darkness takes me.

35: ORION

*Live for the Little Things… When People Fear You,
the Little Things help you Live*

-Ljot

M y mother and her two mates taught me and my six brothers how precious your mate is. I am the youngest of the seven and only the second to find their mate. After my oldest brother found his mate, I always teased him. He softened, especially when she was around. He told me I would understand when I found my mate. I, of course, quoted the statistics telling him how unlikely that was going to be. "You'll See" he would say so sure of himself. Now, watching my mate, I finally understand everything he tried to tell me. The only bad part about this situation is the "I told you so" I was going to get from my brother. It's going to be his new catch phrase anytime I see him.

I smile knowing that I will take his shit any day of the week as long as I get to keep Ori in my life. She is a powerful woman that I am blessed to have. Pride makes my heart swell as I watch her. I love showing her off. When I feel a strange sensation come over me, my smile fades. My body quickly goes numb, confirming my suspicion that something is seriously wrong. I run full speed towards Ori but am still several feet away when she hits the ground. Her head smacks the ground, chin first, bouncing once before finally settling. When I reach Ori, her body is limp. I don't hesitate as I lift her up into my arms and run straight to the med hall, knowing the guys and Lulu will be right behind me. I don't have time to consult them; Ori doesn't have much time left… I can feel it. Storming into the med hall, the previously empty room becomes chaos as the doctor takes one look at Ori.

"What the hell happened?" He asks as he directs me towards the closest bed. I lay her down on the sterile, white cotton sheet. In the short amount of time it took to bring her here from the field, her skin has already gotten paler.

"As soon as she picked up her whip, she collapsed." Cedrick explained from behind me. I watch as Lulu floats the whip past me and laying it on the counter in the back of the room.

"You need to check that." Lulu commands. The medical assistant rushes over without hesitation. We all watch as he swabs the handle and gets straight to work. Within a few seconds he has multiple machines running trying to figure out what was on her talisman. It could be her only chance of survival.

As the minutes tick on, my eyes keep darting between the back of the room and the doctor working on Ori; these are the longest minutes of my life. The doctor's hands are extended over our girl, glowing with his magic. He has his eyes closed in concentration. He needs to go faster. I can feel myself getting weaker, which can only mean one thing. Whatever he is doing right now isn't enough. I look over at the other guys and they are looking pale as well. "She is dying Doc." Barrett says.

"We can feel it." Khalid agrees.

"DO SOMETHING! WE CANNOT LOSE HER!" Cedrick screams at the doctor in frustration. "WE JUST FOUND HER! FIX HER!"

"Doctor Hallswood," the assistant suddenly says with a frantic tone in his voice.

"What is it, son?" the doctor asks.

"Someone poisoned her with Rubycyonide."

"FUCK!" everyone says at the same time. Rubycyonide is a dangerous substance for any Verndari. Once you touch it, it seeps through your pores into your bloodstream and depletes your magical connection and your life force. It is incredibly difficult to remove. Ninety-nine percent of all Verndari who encounter Rubycyonide die. Only someone who has a massive magical connection has any chance of saving our girl.

"Get the Headmaster here NOW!" the doctor commands. The assistant is out of the room before the doctor even finished his sentence.

As we wait, we get weaker and weaker. Our connection letting us know how close she is to dying. When the door finally slams open at the Headmaster's arrival, I am a little relieved. He is the strongest person at the academy. If anyone can save her, he can. I just hope the ten minutes it took to get him doesn't hinder her ability to recover. Rubycyonide makes quick work of us. Every minute is precious.

"What happened?" The Headmaster asks.

"Rubycyonide." We all say, as Barrett and Khalid quickly collapse on the ground, no longer strong enough to stand on their own. Having bonded with Ori already, their quick collapse signifies just how strong their bond is. I force myself to stay conscious until I see the Headmaster starting to work on Ori. By the time my body collapses along-side Barrett and Khalid, my limbs were visibly shaking. As my eyes finally submit to the blackness, Cedrick's body falls with a thud next to mine. All our lives are in the Headmaster's hands now. I just pray he got here in time.

36: ORI.

Every Time Death was Near, I felt like I was being reborn.

-Ljot

The feeling of needles being pulled through my skin is the first sensation I remember. I've lived through a lot during my short life, but nothing compares to the constant pinpricks of pain that are covering my body. For the first time in my life, I'm not afraid to show my pain. When I try to cry out, my body rebels and no sound comes out. Reaching out with my other senses, I search for anything to distract me from my suffering. The sounds of a ticking clock, the water dripping in the faucet, feet pounding down the hallway, none of them are enough to overthrow the feeling of thousands of needles being pulled through my body.

A scream echoes around me, startling me. The feeling of sandpaper in my throat is the only indication that I was the one screaming. As soon as my brain realized that my voice is back, I can't hold back. All the background noise dissipates as my screams intensify, continuing until the last "needle" is pulled through my skin.

All the pain I'm feeling lets me know I'm still alive, but once the pain recedes, I gladly allow the darkness to claim me.

Headmaster:

This day will be forever ingrained into my memory. I've lived hundreds of years and I've never had to attempt what I just did. I can feel the weakness seeping in that only happens when you overuse your magic. It's a feeling that I haven't felt in centuries.

When Ori started screaming, I knew I had done something right. Her screams of pain let us know that she was still alive and fighting; I wouldn't expect anything less from her.

While the others in the medical room, doctors and students alike, were wincing with every scream she made. I used her cries of pain. They spurred me to try harder. I pushed my magic to dig deeper, hunting the poison that was killing her.

When her screams died out, I was confident it was from exhaustion. I knew I had pulled everything out of her system. Now we wait. There is nothing more I can do. With my hands falling to my side, I glance around Medical. The room is crowded with students. Some students are just nosey bastards trying to be an eyewitness to the gossip that will be roaming these halls. Some are genuinely concerned.

The crowd may not have surprised me, but it did piss me off. Normally, I sense others entering, but for the first time since graduating from this school myself, I didn't sense the students from the hallways gathering in the room. I'm sure the students heard her screams from throughout the entire castle, drawing the gathered crowd.

The crowd's eyes are solely on Ori and me. None of them are watching the four additional beds that are pulled up next to her. Khalid, Orion, Barrett, and Cedrick are now laying on them sound asleep. All five of them are pale, but I can safely say that they will all live. When I first entered, I thought I was going to lose them all. Watching them collapse told me just how close to death Ori was.

"Back to what you were doing." I command the crowd, knowing these five don't need an audience. My entire focus shifts to the five lying unconscious in medical. The only indicator that the other students are leaving is the shuffling of their feet.

"Notify me when all five have woken up." I command the doctor once I was sure the audience left.

"Of course, Headmaster." He says right before I shut the door behind me.

37: UNKNOWN

Your Enemies are Usually Closer to You than You Realize

-Ljot

66 "This better be fucking good." I say, furious at being summoned. People don't summon me. I walk into the abandoned tower and my assassin is waiting by the window. He's quiet at first, waiting for me to approach.

"It'll be good. Just watch." He says directing my gaze down to the field below. We have the perfect view of Ori's training. After about ten minutes of watching, even I have to admit that I'm impressed. She is quick study. It isn't until she reaches down and touches her whip that I finally understand what I'm watching. Within seconds, she collapses onto the field.

We've got her this time. I think as a smile graces my face for the first time in 18 years.

The field below us is buzzing with activity. Her mates all rush towards her and one of them scoops her up and runs full speed towards the Medical Hall. The students that were previously standing around gossiping about her power are now standing silent, shocked by the sudden turn of events. Some follow slowly behind, while others start the gossip train that will inevitably result in an unending number of stories regarding Ori's death.

"She will be dead within minutes," my assassin says from next to me. "They will never find her help in time."

"You better be right." I say with a threatening tone. While I am optimistic by the current turn of events, I know better than to celebrate before I see Ori dead with my own eyes.

"We both know that the doctor doesn't have the power to save her. We'll be rid of her and her mates soon." He continues cockily.

We stand in silence as we wait. I have no intention of dismissing him until I know with one hundred percent certainty that he succeeded. We don't have time for another failure. As time drags on, my assassin fidgets next to me. He's aware that Ori should have died by now. The fact that I haven't confirmed her death is making him anxious. But her magical essence is still in the air, I sense it.

I reach out and watch the scene unfold in the Medical hall. Ori is laying pale and immobile on one of the many white beds. At the foot of her bed stands the doctor, impatiently tapping his foot. In the back of the room, Lulu and her men stand with solemn expressions on their faces. Standing next to Ori's prone form, her mates stand watch, getting weaker and weaker as time passes. The color on their skin slowly drains out of them, a sure sign that the

Rubycyonide is doing its job and all five of them will be dead in mere moments.

In this moment, I am optimistic that my assassin's plan succeeded. I wait impatiently for her mates to collapse when the Headmaster suddenly runs in, squashing my optimism right in its tracks. The Headmaster always ruins my plans; why the fuck would this be any different. My anger is so potent, I don't notice Ori's mates collapsing next to her. When I finally notice a pile of her men on the floor next to her bed, it is not enough to quell my anger. As I watched the one person strong enough to save Ori work his magic, my fists clench at my sides till my knuckles are white. My teeth grind together as I watch the last of the Rubycyonide being removed from Ori's body. When the Headmaster's hands fall to his side and the girl's chest is still moving up and down with low shallow breaths, I lose it.

Whipping around, I use my anger to force the would-be assassin up against the wall. He failed again. "YOU FAILED" I screamed at him as I tightened my hold round his throat.

"How?" He asked, genuinely surprised as my hold tightens. He had assumed he had been successful this time; that nothing and no-one here could save her. I lift him up, ensuring his feet are off the ground. He begins kicking and his hands claw at the magic that is still tightening around his throat.

"The Headmaster healed her." I say clenching my teeth together while I spoke.

"How was I supposed to know he could do that? He isn't a healer." He says trying to argue in his favor. "I will try again. I don't fail, you know that." He says barely getting the words out. He is begging for another chance. What he doesn't know is that he is lucky to have gotten a second chance to begin with. I am not known for giving second chances.

"I think I will just take care of it myself." I say as I allow my pressure on his throat to build to the point where he can't breathe. I watched as his face turns blue. I keep my grip on his throat till I know for certain that he can't come back.

Finally releasing him, he falls with a thump to the ground. I walk over and stare at the heap on the ground. *Now what do I do with you?* I think as an idea comes to me. With a flick of the wrist, I send the dead body and the perfect message away.

Now, on to the problem of the girl. There is one sure-fire way to get rid of her without anyone knowing my part in her demise. Wanting to take immediate action, I head out to put my new plans in motion. Plans that won't fail because I won't let them. This girl is as good as dead.

38: RYUU

Emotional Turmoil... an Inevitable Part of Life.

-Ljot

I can hear the thud of her body hitting the ground from across the field. You can see everyone visibly wince when Ori hit the ground. Without asking, we all know something is terribly wrong. My heart is immediately pulled in two different directions. I'm conflicted. While I haven't known Ori long, she is family now. I am torn between following my family and ensuring her safety and staying out here to investigate.

All the missions they have sent me on over the years give me insight into what is happening to her, and it fucking pisses me off. She's been put through more pain and torment than anyone I know. She needs time to heal physically, mentally, and emotionally. Instead of getting that time, she has someone trying to kill her and unfortunately, they might have succeeded this time. If it ends up being what I think it is, her odds of survival are extremely low. We can count the number of Verndari that have survived it on one hand.

Now I have to choose between being there for my brother, who in a matter of minutes will collapse right along with Ori's other mates or try catching the bastard that keeps trying to kill her. My heart is in a game of tug-of-war and for the first time in my life I'm unsure of which side is going to win.

"We have to catch the bastard" Dain says from next to me. His anger as prominent as my own.

"What about Cedrick?" I ask, needing his opinion on whether we need to go to our brother first.

"He'd want us to catch the bastard." Dain says bluntly and with hatred in his voice. "If he comes out of this and finds out that we were merely pacing medical the entire time, he will rip us a new one. I wouldn't blame him either. We need to find the bastard for him."

We remain on the sidelines of the field, watching until the last of Ori's Mate's rush off. I only allow myself those few seconds to process our reality before forcing myself into work mode; flipping the switch in my mind that buries my emotions.

As soon as that flip is switched, my mind immediately starts thinking up all feasible options. How did someone get close enough to her whip? I storm off the field with Dain at my heels to the location that makes the most sense... our bedroom. They were staying there last night. Someone getting in while they were sleeping is the most logical explanation for how her whip got tainted. If we don't find any clues there, we will have to speak with Ori directly. I'm hoping it doesn't come to that; if she lives, she will be unconscious for a while.

The walk to our room is quiet and somber; both of us deep in our own thoughts. When we make it to the door, Dain does his thing. If you were looking at him, you would see his hands in the air, eyes closed and crunched up in concentration, with wrinkles forming on his forehead. He is in his zone. A zone that you can't shake him out of. Your only option is to wait till he comes out of his own accord.

"What the FUCK?" He screams as his arms drop. "There is no unknown signature."

"What the hell does that mean?" Not expecting an actual answer. That doesn't make sense.

"The only people who have entered our rooms in the last few days are Ori, her mates, and our team. That's it." He says dumbfounded, as stumped by that development as I am.

I slowly open that door and enter the main living rooms. Nothing is out of place; everything laying exactly as we left it. Knowing we won't find anything in there, I walk straight for the bedroom and pray we have better luck in there.

"Did you call for Gylfi?" I asked Dain.

"Yeah, I told him to meet us here, but he didn't respond." Dain tells me.

"Where the hell are you, Gylfi?" I mumble to myself. We need all hands-on deck. This isn't the time for a team member to go missing. It's too important.

Seconds later, Gylfi, a man I consider a brother, appears at my feet. His skin is pale, and his lips are blue. You can see bruises forming around his throat where someone choked him. Laying on his chest is a note:

>Ryuu, Dain, and Cedrick,
>
>I'm surprised that you would call this man your brother. He betrayed you quite easily; it didn't take much convincing. He was more interested in power and money than your brotherhood. Unfortunately for him, he failed me. I gave him two chances, and he failed. He was lucky I gave a second chance; I don't give second chances.
>
>I was told he was the best. His performance these last few days has been disappointing. Was he really the best? Probably not, considering he failed at getting rid of Ori. Yes, your brother tried to Kill Ori.
>
>Cedrick, how does it feel to know that your brother was the one trying to kill your mate? I wish I was there to see your face. If you really want to know what your brother was capable of, run his magical signature against all your unsolved cases. I think you'll be surprised by what you find.
>
>Yours Truly
>
>P.S. Tell Ori I'm coming for her.

"Holy Shit" Dain exclaims, taking the words right out of my mouth. "Do you think it is true?" He asks, shock lacing his voice.

"I fucking hope not, but we can't rule it out. He could have easily gained access to the bedroom while Ori was here. Run his signature against the dead bomb." I command. "If it's a match, we will have our answer."

Dain quickly walks away to find the answers we seek. I know it won't take him long. Dain is one of the best; his speed and accuracy are legendary among our kind. No one questions his results. Our team depends on his skills, and we wouldn't be nearly as good without him.

When I hear Dain swearing behind me, I know what the results are before he tells me. "It was him, wasn't it?"

"Yes, sir."

"Take care of the body." I command. "Once you do that, find out how many of our open cases were executed by him. I'm going to medical so I can wait for Cedrick to wake up. I don't want him to hear the news from anyone else." How the hell do I break this kind of news to him?

39: HEADMASTER

What Some see as a Weakness is in reality your Greatest Strength

-Ljot

I'm still weak when I'm called by the other Council members. I hate for them to see me weak. Saving Ori took most of my magic; I haven't felt this drained since I first gained my powers. My pasty white skin and low energy levels will be sure signs to them all that I have drained myself. I only have the walk from medical to my office to mentally prepare for what I know is coming.

When I open my office door, I am silently hoping my office is empty. My wishes did not become reality. The rest of the Council has arrived and are standing around my desk talking amongst themselves.

"How is everyone?" I ask as I walk around them to my place behind my ornate wooden desk.

"Better than you by the looks of it." Someone mumbled.

"Why the sudden visit?" I ask, unwilling to let their snide comments get the better of me.

"Always straight to the point. I have always liked that about you." the councilwoman says. "The trial will commence tomorrow."

I nod my head. I expected another trial. We typically have a trial every 6 months or so, but it's been about 9 months since the last one. Cora and Lillia are both expected to have their trial; they've had more training with their mates than most get. "Who is going in?" I question, unsure if their intention is to have a single or double trial. Wouldn't be the first time we completed a double trial; it's just been a while.

"Ori" the oldest of us states. I silently curse in my head. I should've expected this. As soon as they realized the strength she possesses, they would have started their plotting. They have always been afraid of those that hold more power than them. She threatens their very existence. Stupid fucking bastards.

"She was just poisoned and hasn't woken up yet. Expecting her to go through a trial is ridiculous. She might not even be awake by tomorrow morning. Cora and Lillia have been here much longer, put them through their trial." I state trying to sway their option to the logical decision that is based on facts... not fear.

"Cora and Lillia can wait for their trial. It's Ori's time." They reiterate adamantly, like it is perfectly normal to initiate a trial after a week of training.

"You need to give Ori more time. Give her at least a few days to heal. Considering we haven't been able to keep her safe, it's the least we can do." I argue with them. Using logic to sway them is my usual strategy, but I will resort to begging if I have to. I need to get her more time. Ori and her men will never be able to show for a trial in the morning; there's a very good chance she'll still be unconscious. Unfortunately, if they don't show up for their trial, they forfeit. The consequences of forfeiting are deadly... literally.

"How long before she wakes?" The Councilwoman asks. She's the only one on the Council that has some semblance of empathy; even she has to dig deep to find it.

"48 hours" I say giving my best guess. I may have exaggerated the timing a bit.

"3 days." The councilwoman says. "We will give them 3 days to start the trial. After that they forfeit."

"Thank you, councilwoman. I will inform them as soon as they wake."

The others reluctantly nod their heads at me before quietly leaving the room. I wait until the door slams shut behind them to start cursing. The distinct bang of the door sounds, igniting the fury I was hiding. "Fucking bastards!" I scream at the top of my lungs.

Ori and her mates should be given time to heal, but that isn't a luxury they have. I immediately go back to medical. When I arrive, the doctor is silently watching all five of them. Ori is laying in a hospital bed in the far corner of the room, with her mates in beds lining the wall between her and the door.

"How long before they are awake?" I ask him.

"Ori will probably be awake soon." He says shocking me.

"How? That shouldn't be possible."

"Her mates are healing her. I've only ever read about this phenomenon. It's incredible. I can see their magic slowly gliding through the room over to her. None of the men have healed any. Their bodies are literally putting her first. I never thought I'd ever get the opportunity to see this." The doctor says in wonderment. I understand his fascination and any other day, I would grill him with questions, but right now there are more important things.

"Get me as soon as they wake up. Their trial has to start within the next 72 hours."

"But Headmaster ..." He says arguing with me. I cut him off before he can even finish his sentence.

"Not my fucking choice, Doc... definitely not my choice. All we can do now is wake them as quick as possible and prepare them for what is to come. The rest is in their hands." I say solemnly. "I just pray they are strong enough to overcome this." I finish.

I know how strong all five of them are, but with so little time to train, I question even their ability to get through the trial. It will be a miracle if they survive.

Ori:

It's dark out when I finally open my eyes. At first, I panic. I feel my breathing become erratic when nothing looks familiar. My pulse jumps, but as I take in my surroundings, it's obvious that I'm in some sort of medical wing. Between the microscopes and test tubes, combined with the white sheets lying over me, and twin beds on the other side of the room, it's the only conclusion I could draw. But...

Where are my guys? Why aren't they here? I think. Disappointment seeping into my bones. We have been growing closer as of late, and I was beginning to believe that they wouldn't abandon me. *But they* have. My head tells me as tears fall down my cheeks.

"They haven't abandoned you." A deep fatherly voice informs me from the far side of the room. The man in question has black rings under his eyes, telling me he hasn't slept in a while. His grey and white aging hair a sign of his long life. He is wearing white robes, solidifying my belief that I am in a medical center of some sort. "They are laying right next to you." He tells me, motioning to my right with a small smile on his face.

I turn in the direction he pointed out and gasp. My men are pale. If I wasn't seeing their chest moving up and down, I would have thought they had died.

"What happened to them?" I asked.

"Your connection to them is strong. Stronger than I would've expected after such a short period of time." He says.

"What does our connection have to do with anything?" I ask. He sighs, frustrated by my lack of knowledge. "I know my knowledge is limited, but I want to learn and understand." I tell him honestly.

"For mates, when your connection is powerful enough, your mates will sense and feel when you are suffering. Usually, they simply feel when you are in pain. It helps them take care of you. Rarely, the connection is strong enough between the female and her mates that they are all destined to die at the same time. It is a rare thing to see. You are incredibly lucky."

"LUCKY!" I scream. "I don't want them to die." I whisper, tears pooling in my eyes yet again.

"That's the beautiful thing ..." He starts. "As long as you live… they live. But as soon as you pass, they will follow. Right now, your mates are weak. They were helping to heal you. I've never seen anything like it. Even in their sleep, you came first. I could sense their energy going to you. Give them time, they will be awake in no time." He finishes.

I stare at my mates, willing them to wake up. I don't know how long I just watch them, but my impatience gets the better of me and soon I find myself climbing out of bed. I'm weak at first, but my stubborn determination gets the better of me. I push all four of their beds together, needing all five of us to be near.

I expect the doctor to stop me. Tell me to rest and heal, but he doesn't. I do however hear a distinct laugh from the far corner of the room. When all four beds are finally together, I climb in and lay down in-between the four of them, carefully positioning myself so I am touching them all. In no time, I find myself falling into a peaceful sleep.

40: CEDRICK

Experiencing Limbo is a Blessing and a Curse

-Ljot

Collapsing is imminent. I feel myself getting weaker and weaker as Ori's heart slows. I get a brief glimpse of the Headmaster attempting to save Ori's life right before darkness consumes me.

For hours, I found myself in limbo. It's a place that most people hear about, but never see. Having a mate close to death is the only circumstance that brings you to limbo. Here, my mind is connected to the other guys; we were all in limbo together. Their magical signatures are a calming presence. This place is a halfway between reality and death; a bus stop right before we move on. The only images I see are the magical signatures around me. Everything else is a foggy haze.

Physically, I still feel everything. Currently, my magic is buzzing under my skin and I feel it slowly draining. My magic has a mission, protecting the woman it loves. I would willingly die 10 times over if it meant saving the woman I love. I watch as the magic from the other men reach the same destination, Ori. We are all protecting her.

Time seems to stop as my body works to help heal her; I have no sense of how much time has passed. The tension under my skin tightens until the moment my magic senses that she will be okay. The energy I was using to stay conscious while in limbo drains from my body the moment I knew she would live. Within seconds, my body succumbs to the last remnants of darkness.

The next time I wake up, I find Ori laying across me and the guys. She looks so peaceful like this, although her position is rather awkward. She positioned herself so she could touch all four of us: her head is laying on my chest, her hands are holding onto Barrett and Khalid who are currently resting on either side of me, and her feet are wrapped around Orion's thighs. You can hear her soft snores as she rests on us.

"You guys awake?" I ask quietly, hoping they made it back to the land of the living. If they weren't with me yet, I knew they would be soon.

"Yes. I feel like I was run over by a truck." Orion groans as the door to medical suddenly opens. I am not surprised to see the Headmaster. This man knows everything, so it doesn't shock me that he is aware we have awoken.

"About damn time." He grumbles, coming to stand at the foot of our beds.

"How long were we out?" I ask.

"Too fucking long." You can see the tension in his shoulders as he says this.

"What happened?" I ask, suddenly afraid to know the answer.

"You guys have 54 hours left before you have to start your trail. If you don't start within that time, you forfeit."

"What the HELL!" Khalid exclaims loud enough to make Ori stir.

"It wasn't my decision, Khalid." The Headmaster says, defending himself. "I bought you as much time as I could. Trust me, I tried for longer, but the others on the Council wouldn't have it. I got you 72 hours. You slept for 18 of those hours."

"She won't be ready in 54 hours. She'll still be weak for at least 24 of those." Barrett says as he looks down at our girl.

"You guys need to make her ready. You all know the consequences of forfeiting."

"What do you suggest?" I ask. Knowing the Headmaster, he already has a plan in that head of his. It's a rare day for him to not have a plan; he is a very strategic individual.

"You take her and go to the special training rooms. I'll let you out when you have an hour left. This will maximize your training and keep her abilities a secret from anyone who might be watching. It should also help protect her from any more attempts on her life. The less those bastards who design the trials know, the better. And then when you go into the trials, you pray."

"She is going to need Lulu. She is Ori's best shot at getting out of this alive." I tell the Headmaster.

"I can let Lulu and her men in, but no one else can know that you are down there."

I nod my head in complete agreement; the less people know of our plans, the better chance Ori has. I look down at her still peacefully sleeping and I caress her hair. I'd love to let her keep sleeping, but at the moment, that is not an option. The sky outside is dark and most people in the school are tucked away in their rooms. Leaving now to the special training room is our best chance of getting there without anyone else knowing.

"Rise and shine, sweetheart. We have to go." I say, trying to coax her awake. Her head whips up and looks at me. She smiles brightly and then looks around for the others. When she sees that we are all awake, tears flow down her cheeks.

"You are all okay. I thought I lost you, but you are okay." She says just barely above a whisper.

"We aren't leaving you anytime soon, sweetheart." I tell her reassuringly.

"I hate to break up the reunion, but you guys really have to go. People are going to wake up in about an hour and we have to get you there before then." The Headmaster says, reminding me why I woke her up to begin with.

"Where are we going?" Ori asks.

"I'll explain when we get there." I tell her, "But we have to move now." I finish trying to convey the importance of leaving; time isn't on our side right now.

Ori watches me. I don't know what she is looking for, but her eyes shine with all the trust in the world. I can tell she trusts us completely, which makes my heart shine brighter for her. It doesn't take a genius to realize that she does not give out trust easily. The life she has lived gives her every right to questions us and keep her trust tucked away in a dark corner, never to be given out. But our woman is strong and resilient and has already given us her trust freely.

"Well then, what are we waiting for?" Ori asks as she climbs out of the beds. She is up in a blink of an eye, just waiting for us to follow. That's my girl.

41: ORI

The Closer you are to your Mates, the Stronger your Bond will be

-Ljot

The five of us followed the Headmaster deep into the school. By the time we reach our destination we had gone down 5 flights; I didn't even know that was possible. The whole last flight was pitch black, making it difficult to see. He brings us to two large metal double doors. I have seen nothing like them. Next to the door, I see Lulu and her men are waiting for us. Lulu has quickly become my best friend. Having her there puts me at ease; other than my men, she is the only one I trust.

Stopping in front of the doors, the Headmaster waves his hands in a crisscross pattern causing the doors to slide open allowing us entrance. The screech of the metal door on the floor lets me know how heavy these doors are. The Headmaster steps aside and ushers us in. Other than the Headmaster, everyone enters the room as if this was a normal, everyday occurrence.

Stepping in, I didn't really know what to expect, but it definitely wasn't what I found. The room is a strange mixture of a living area and a training room. On the right side there are dummies, exercise equipment, targets, and even a rope course. On the left is a living area. There are two massive beds, a table, and a kitchen area. In the back is a small door that I'm hoping leads to the bathroom.

"Ori, you are going to need this." The Headmaster says from behind me. I turn around and he has my whip in his hands. I hesitate to take it from him. "Don't worry, it's been cleaned and sanitized. I made sure all the poison was removed from it myself." He states as I reluctantly reach out to grab it from him. When my hand closes around the handle and nothing happens, I release the breath I didn't know I was holding.

"I know it might not seem like it now, but I really am doing everything I can to protect you." The Headmaster tells me. "I will be back in 54 hours to come get you, then you will start your trial. Use this time wisely." He says calmly right before he leaves and locks us in the room. At his words, panic immediately sets in.

"Why the hell do I have my trial already?" I ask, screeching. I have only known about magic for a week, I shouldn't have a trial already. Why haven't the other girls had their trial? They certainly have been here longer than me. I look to the guys for an answer, but they are having a silent conversation amongst themselves.

Lulu, my always truthful and blunt friend, is the one that approaches me first. "I am going to be blunt here, Ori." She says looking me right in the eyes. "They are afraid of you. Those in power don't want you around and they feel the best way to get rid of you without having to get their hands dirty would be to allow the trial to kill you for them. But we aren't going to allow that to happen." Lulu says with sympathy in her eyes. "We are going to do everything we can in the next 54 hours to get you not only prepared but ready to complete the trial and get the hell out of dodge."

By this point, I have tears forming in my eyes. I have spent my entire life fighting. I don't want to fight anymore. Lulu grabs onto my hands, then looks me square in the eyes. "You can fight one more time. You pass the trial, and they can't touch you." She says. "Are you ready to be the fighter that we all know you are?"

I can't speak, I just nod my head. "Good." She says smiling at me. "Now to get to the important question ... who do you still have to have sex with?" I immediately blush and look up at my men, my eyes going between Orion and Cedrick.

Lulu, being the observant person that she is, watches my eyes. "Cedrick and Orion… huh… Go get them." She urges with a smirk before she turns towards her own men. I watch her as she brings her men over to the bed that's up against the wall. I watch her as she unabashedly undresses for her men, right in front of us. I know I should look away, but I can't.

Orion and Cedrick both stalk towards me and stand on either of my sides. "You like watching them… don't you?" Cedrick whispers in my ear so softly that I am surprised I even heard him.

"Yes." I admit shocking myself.

"I don't think they'll care if you watch." Cedrick says as he guides me towards the other bed. We end up on the side of our own bed, giving me a view of everything that Lulu and her men do. Orion and Cedrick both take a side of my shirt and carefully lift it over my head. My breasts fall free as soon as the shirt is lifted over my head.

Cedrick carefully pushes me down at my waist. My chest is laying on the bed, while my ass is in the air and my feet are still firmly planted on the ground. "Keep your eyes on them, Ori." Cedrick commands as I feel him slip my pants and panties down my legs. I lift my head at his command and rest my chin on the bed, keeping my eyes on Lulu. As soon as the last of my clothes are gone, I feel a finger enter me briefly before it is pulled back out. "Our little Voyeur." Orion says as he finds out how wet I already am. I can hear the smirk in his voice as he says it. "She just loves watching. Look how wet she already is." I can picture him showing Cedrick his wet finger. "She tastes delicious too." Cedrick says making me whimper as I picture him licking my juices off Orion's finger.

A dip in the bed told me someone was joining me on the bed. In my peripheral vision, I can see Barrett and Khalid on either side on my head. Their dicks out and they are slowly stroking themselves with one hand. Their other hands grab onto my hair pulling it tight forcing my head off the bed. "Don't even think about closing your eyes." Khalid commands.

In front of me, I watch as Lulu is on her hands and knees. Her tits are being suckled by one of her men as he enters her pussy from underneath her. Another man is grabbing the lube and I instantly whimper, well aware of what I am going to be watching.

In that instant, I feel one of my men enter me. Holding my hips tight, he slams into me. I feel him pulling in and out. Between the sensation of his cock moving in me and watching Lulu, it doesn't take long for me to go crashing over the cliff, screaming in ecstasy. As my pussy tightens on the dick inside me, I feel the heat of his seed release inside of me.

My eyes close in that moment of their own accord. The minute they do, my hair is pulled tighter, causing my eyes to snap open. "Watch them, Ori" Barrett commands.

Lulu now has both men inside of her, one in her pussy while the other is in her anus. If her moans are any indication, they are both pounding into her with a ferocity that she enjoys.

My attention goes back to my pussy as it suddenly feels empty, but not for long. Soon there is another dick inside of me. I feel cherished as someone leans forward, a chiseled chest touching my back. It is slower this time; they are drawing out everything I feel, bringing me to the brink and back again. He keeps going until Lulu collapses in a pile of her men.

When I no longer have a scene to watch, he pulls up from my back and finally allows himself to let go. Within seconds he is exploding deep inside of me and I orgasm with him, milking his cock.

Barrett and Khalid are still next to my head and they take that moment to shoot their load on the top of my back, marking me in their own way. My head collapses as soon as they let go of my hair. My eyes closing of their own accord.

I feel someone pick me up and put me gently into the center of the bed. "Sleep Ori. You're going to need your energy." Cedrick says as he settles next to me. It isn't until the last of my men settle on the bed that I finally allow myself the sleep my body craves.

42: RYUU

Life is Full of Surprises... Enjoy them

-Ljot

D ain and I have been taking turns standing
guard outside of medical. I don't like how
vulnerable they are right now. I've seen
enough evil to recognize how it's an ideal time for the
killer to strike again. We're going to make sure that
doesn't happen.

When the Headmaster finally makes another
appearance, I perk up. They are awake; it's the only
explanation. I wait impatiently with my foot tapping
the floor. Ten minutes later, the Headmaster leaves
medical with all five of the following closely behind.

I suspect I know where he is leading them; it's
probably the only safe place in this school. I need to
know for sure, so as soon as they were out of sight,
my magic reached out and I watch through the
Headmaster's eyes. It's a trick of mine that I rarely
have to access, but right now I am grateful for. While
most individuals are not strong enough to sense my
presence, the Headmaster is a different story. Within
seconds of entering his vision, I could tell he knew I

was there. He could have easily kicked me out. I was grateful he let me stay until the doors shut behind them, sealing them safely away behind the solid doors.

"They are safe. Now get out of my head." The Headmaster says to me, irritation coating his voice. Knowing they are safe, I willingly leave.

"What did you find out?" I asked Dain, sensing that he was now next to me.

"Gylfi was not the person we thought. He was using us."

I sigh, knowing what was coming was going to be bad. "How many cases? How many years?" I asked Dain.

"75 percent of our unsolved cases since he joined our team 40 years ago." I look him in the eye, and wait, knowing that I'm not going to like what I hear. "42 cases." He finally sums up.

"They were all the Red gem cases... weren't they?" I ask as my voice rising in pitch. I couldn't even hide my anger anymore. Dain just nods his head. "The Red Gem Assassin was right under our noses all those years. How the hell did I not realize it was him? I should have fucking seen it?" I am pissed at myself. Being the leader, it's my job to know my men. If I had known it was him, I would have saved so many lives. Instead, I let him play with us for forty fucking years.

"None of us saw it Ryuu." Dain tries to reassure me. "What do you want to do now? We have to figure out who's after Ori. Not only for her sake, but for Cedrick's as well."

"Whoever it is has to be powerful. It's the only explanation for how they got into the school undetected and killed Gylfi." Dain nods his head. I can tell he isn't sure where my thoughts are headed. "Who are the only Verndari strong enough to pull off these tasks undetected?" I ask Dain. I instantly see the lightbulb going off in his head.

"The Council" He says shock still on his face. "But who?"

Unknown:

The shattering of glass echoes around the room. When my temper got the best of me, my magic automatically flared sending the few vases and other knick-knacks that I have in my office hurling across the room. They all shattered into thousands of little pieces. At my age, my control should never allow my magic to flare due to my anger. But as soon as I heard the Headmaster moved Ori to the one-place I couldn't reach her, my magic snapped. It's as unhappy as I was that we've failed more in the last few days than we have in years.

"AHHHHHHH" I scream, needing to release the anger that is starting to consume me.

If the fucking Headmaster hadn't locked them in that room, my plans wouldn't have been ruined. I knew I should have gone after them while they were in medical. I held back though knowing that Ryuu and Dain probably expected a move like that. But that locked room is the only place in the entire school where I can't reach them. He designed the room himself as a safe haven. The Council has tried to gain access, but he always refused to give us the information saying the less people that knew, the safer people would be in the event it needed to be used.

When it became obvious that the Headmaster wasn't going to relent, I made it my personal mission to figure out how to access it. Through the years, I have made multiple attempts to get in and have failed every time. The fucking bastard is smarter than I first gave him credit for.

Needing to focus on what I can control, I walk over to my plans for Ori's trial. They are laid out across my desk. Right now, her trial already has three obstacles. I added as much as I could while trying to ensure the others don't get too suspicious.

In its current state, Ori only has about 30 percent chance of making it out alive. Since another hit on her prior to her trial isn't an option, I glance through all the Obstacles and look for improvements. I need insurance that she won't make it out of the trials alive.

Just a little tweak here and there, I think, as I make the obstacles harder and harder throughout her trial. By the time I am done, it is by far the hardest trial we have ever put anyone through. Just what I wanted. It doesn't matter how strong her men are, she won't make it out alive.

43: ORI

Physical Strength is a Fundamental Component to Magical Strength

-Ljot

I'm exhausted. With only five hours left before we start the trials, I am finally given a reprieve from training. Lulu told me to get some rest "cause I'm going to need it." Her words, not mine. That woman is a beast; I admire her, but right now I am not her biggest fan. I currently don't have the energy to walk, so I'll take a nap right here on the floor. The floor mat is actually comfortable, I think, as my eyes shut.

40 hours Earlier:

I was shaken awake after only a few hours of sleep. Lulu and her men were already waiting on us. Lulu looked like her perky badass self. I, on the other hand, still felt very weak and looked like a mess. I was lucky that they gave me a few minutes to clean up. "Five minutes" she said as I head straight for the shower. The shower stall is a basic one-person shower; it reminds me of the shower stall in my foster family's house, just nicer. As soon as I turn the shower on, hot water cascades down my skin and I enjoy every minute of it. I walk out feeling refreshed but am stopped dead in my tracks by Lulu's piercing eyes; I took too long. She thrust a protein bar into my hands the second I came out of the bathroom; apparently there is no time for breakfast. She immediately leads me to the ropes course that I've been dreading since our arrival. Couldn't we just skip this part.

I've never seen anything like this monstrosity. Looking up, I see small platforms about ten feet up that are barely big enough for you to balance on, there are ropes hanging from the ceiling, netting set up like a vertical wall, and large hoops. Underneath the course are large mats meant to buffer your fall.

I spend the next few hours just trying to get through the course without falling. I wish I could say I completed it on my first attempt, but that would be a lie. After falling twenty-seven times, I finally make it through without falling. I'm hoping that's it, but once Lulu was sure I perfected the course, she made me run the damn thing with magic being shot at me. Apparently... I needed to practice my reflexes. It sucked. I got hit so much I lost count. Lucky for me, the guys could heal me... cue sarcasm. I love being healed just so I could be tortured all over again.

When I wasn't working on the ropes course, I was perfecting my hand to hand combat, and how I could use my magic in a fight. That was probably the hardest part. I only had enough control for the basics, so everyone took turns teaching me unique ways of using those skills. With so many people helping, I learned some unique skills that I pray will come in useful during the trial. The longer I kept

practicing my magic, the more drained I felt. Until
eventually I knew I didn't have any more magic in me.

Present:

My eyes remained close as I feel myself being
lifted up by one of my men.
"Go ahead and sleep, Ori. We got you."
Cedrick whispers. I barely caught his words before I
willingly fell asleep in his arms.

Khalid:

The entire room is silent as we watch Cedrick
lift Ori off the ground, setting her on the bed. I know
she is exhausted. Over the past few days, she has
gotten maybe 6 hours of sleep. We couldn't spare any
more time. There is just too much as stake. I watched,
proud as fuck of her, until she finally collapsed on the
mat. In that moment, we all knew her body was done.
So, for the next 5 hours she can sleep and then we face
fate.
When Cedrick comes back. Barrett leaves
without a word and lays down next to her, pulling
her close. He positions himself so that her back is to
his chest and his arm is wrapped around her waist,
holding her tight up against him. I'm not surprised by
his actions. He is trying to heal her and help her

magic rejuvenate. I haven't known him long, but he wasn't going to be able to just sit here while she suffers.

"He's going to need his energy just as much as Ori." Lulu points out in a whisper. "I'm not sure that is a smart idea."

"You wouldn't have been able to stop him." Orion says. "Honestly, if he didn't go, I would have. It's killing us to see her like this; I'm sure you understand."

"We understand completely." Lulu's mates say simultaneously. "One of us would have done the same if it was Lulu. I just hope that 5 hours is enough."

"Me too." I whisper. "Me too."

Ori:

When I am woken up, I feel more alive that I have in a while. Next to me, Barrett pulls me close and gives me a quick kiss. When I pull back, I get a good look at him and I notice how pale he looks. He has dark circles beginning to form under his eyes, like he hasn't slept in a while.

"What's wrong, Barrett?" I ask.

"Nothing's wrong." He starts as he softly caresses my cheek. When I give him my I don't believe you look, he continues. "I just gave some of my magical energy to you; you need to be at your best."

"BARRETT..." I start but am quickly cut off.

"I can't lose you, Ori. None of us can lose you. We just found you." He finishes with tears in his eyes.

"I'm going to fight for all of us, Barrett. I'm not leaving you." I say confidently. Over the last few weeks, these men have become the family I've always wanted. They are my home and I have no intention of losing them.

"Well, that's good news, cause it's time." The Headmaster suddenly says, making me jump. I feel my heart race as I look over at him and nod my head. I look for my men and find the others standing by the door, waiting. Smiles full of faith showing on their faces.

Barrett holds my hand as we walk towards the others. When we reach them, Orion grabs my other hand; I feel safer with my men surrounding me. Their presence allows my heart to calm and my mind to focus.

As we begin our walk to the dreaded trial, I say my mantra in my head over and over again. *I can do this. I am a strong, powerful woman. No one is going to stop me from having a family.* I'm not giving up my only chance at happiness for a madman.

44: ORI

Small Moments in Time Change your Life

-Ljot

I can barely see the individual walking in front of me. Since the hallway is pitch black with no windows, I suspect we are deep underground. It only takes us a few turns before we make it to a stairwell. The stairs curve in a spiral up five flights before I see a glimpse of daylight. At the top of the stairs, a thick oak door blocks most of the light. The sun is seen peeking in from a small crack at the bottom of the door. The door creaks when the Headmaster opens it. Blinding light immediately hits my eyes causing my eyes to instinctually slam them shut.

Running into Lulu's back, an umph escapes me. The normal bustling noise of the school abruptly stops at our arrival. All eyes are on me as the students line the walls all up and down the corridor. They leave a path down the center for us like they knew we were coming. The Headmaster only pauses for a second before continuing in what feels like a funeral procession. The looks the student give are a strange mix of curiosity and pity. I do my best to ignore them. I don't need any of their looks in my head right now.

Leaving the main building of the school, the Headmaster guides us past the practice fields and turns the corner. In the back sits what looks like an old colosseum. When we walk in, I'm faced with the strangest sight I have ever seen. It is a strange mix of old, new, and magical. The building itself is made of old stone, giving it an ancient feel. In the stands, there's metal bench seating that clashes with the overall look of the building. High in the sky, there are large circular purple orbs that are all around the colosseum. The magical orbs lighting up the entire building.

"Your trial is projected onto the orbs so that everyone can watch." Barrett says from next to me, having noticed what has caught my attention.

We're brought all the way to the far end, where an old stone arch stands tall. The arch is made of stone that matches the colosseum walls. Between the sides of the arch, a purple magical signature matching the magical orbs above our heads shimmers, creating what looks like a magical doorway. I'm so engrossed in the weird arch that I failed to realize people were taking their seats.

"Once you enter, trust you heart, trust your instincts, and trust your men. You get through this and they can't control you anymore." Lulu says after she turns around and looks me in the eye.

"Lulu, be honest ... what are my odds?" I ask.

"Your odds don't matter. You can do this. Besides, you won't make me lose my best friend, are you?" she asks.

"No." I answer with a genuine smile on my face. Having a friend waiting for me is a bright spot in my unknown future. She grabs onto my shoulders, giving me a reassuring squeeze before heading away with her guys.

"You ready?" Khalid asks.

"No." I answer honestly. "But I don't really have a choice, do I?"

"We will get through this together. Just trust your instincts." He says reiterating what Lulu said before grabbing a hold of a hand and walking me toward the archway. With my men by my side, I walk right through the purple archway to my unknown future. For the next few hours, I will force myself to focus on what I can control and hope it will be enough to get me to the future I have dreamed of.

Walking though the barrier my body tingles slightly before we end up standing on top of a cliff with a drop off just feet away. If you look down, there's no bottom in sight. *Don't fall… Don't fall…* I think, before I back up slightly only to find a solid wall at my back. The ledge we are standing on is a foot and a half wide, just large enough for us to stand on. In front of us is a wide abyss with a few stone pillars scattered around, fog sits just below the edge making it impossible to see how tall they stand. In the sky, phoenixes are flying around looking like they are ready to pounce on anything that comes their way.

You can see flames flickering throughout the sky as far as the eye can see.

"I count ten." Khalid says from next to me.

"Are you sure that's all?" I ask. Something tells me there's more that we can't see.

"How the hell did they get phoenixes?" Orion asks, shock evident in his tone.

"The most I have ever seen is 3." Cedrick says, also shocked at the situation we currently find ourselves in. "The larger flock, the more dangerous they are. They aren't seen co-existing in groups larger than 4."

"What the hell are we going to do?" I ask at a complete loss on what to do. I know absolutely nothing about phoenixes.

"It's your trial, Ori. You're our leader. What are we going to do?" Khalid asks.

Good fucking question.

45: ORI

Enjoy Every Minute of Life

-Ljot

W e stand watching the beautiful fiery birds as I ponder our first move. As a test, I take my whip out and lash it towards the closest bird. As soon as the whip snaps in front of its face, the phoenix rears back and turns in our direction. As an obvious expression of anger, a fireball is flung in our direction.

I shove Khalid and Cedrick pushing them further down the ledge; Barrett and Orion are following fast at my heals. The shattering of the wall behind us comes seconds before a slight burning sensation starts on my back. FUCK! Turning around, I find Orion crumbled on the small ledge behind Barrett. Orion is barely balanced on the ledge with his right arm and leg dangling off. His shirt is burnt off his back; there is hardly any fabric left. His upper back is covered in red blisters from the phoenix's fire. While I can already see it healing, it will scar.

"I am so sorry." I say as tears fall down my cheeks. "It's all my fault." I whisper.

"I will be fine." Orion says barely above a whisper as he groans. I wince as he stands back on his feet. "Let's just not do that again."

I need to get us out of here, I think, as I look back out at the abyss in front of us. The space between us and the first pillar is too far to get to on our own; besides, it is too small for all of us, so that won't work. Suddenly a light bulb goes off in my head. *I'm not sure the guys are going to like this.*

I wait patiently with whip in hand, allowing my magic to flow through it. My magic flares inside me, lighting up my whip with my signature red glow. As soon as one of the phoenixes gets close enough, I let my whip fly and wrap it around the phoenix's neck. Within seconds of contact, I push images of us playing together when we were both young into the phoenix's memory. I let the memories develop naturally, linking us together like family. To the phoenix, a bond is formed that can never be broken. She is a beautifully protective soul… my beautifully protective soul. She flies back towards me. When she gets close enough, I leap from the ledge onto her back. I hear the screams of my guys sounding through the air. Their relief that I'm safe sits heavily inside me. I look up in their direction and smile before I fly out to get my men their own phoenixes to ride.

Orion:

I love her dearly, but she is crazy. Crazy in the best possible way. Who the hell would've thought to ride the Phoenix? That wasn't a thing. Since when is that a thing? I guess it is now.

We all watch stunned as she flies around among the phoenixes as if she belongs there. When she gets to the largest of the phoenixes, her whip wraps around its neck and her magic does its work. Both Phoenixes are hovering in the air. Slowly, the flames of the largest phoenix die down to a safe level. I don't know how she is managing it, but she is taming the beasts. When her whip drops from its neck, it flies towards us and stops right in front of Khalid. He jumps, landing safely on his back, and rides off on his own phoenix.

One by one I watch as Cedrick and Barrett both also get their own Phoenix, leaving me alone on the cliff. When the final Phoenix comes up, it hovers right in front of me waiting.

"Hop on." Ori suddenly urges from behind the waiting phoenix. "She won't hurt you… I promise." Ori says with so much faith.

"How do you know?" I question, still hesitant. I trust Ori, but the throbbing pain of the burn on my back makes me hesitant to ride a Phoenix at the moment; being burnt by one will do that to a man. Pardon me for being reluctant.

I immediately regret questioning her. For a brief moment, pain flashes in Ori's eyes.

"I formed a bond between you and her. She will never hurt you. From now on, she'll always protect you." She says in a whisper that I barely hear over the flapping of the Phoenixes wings.

"I'm sorry about your back. It's all my fault." She says, a tear slipping out of her eye.

"It's not your fault, sweetheart." I say honestly. I need her to believe the truth in my words. She smiles slightly at me before motioning for me to get on the back of the Phoenix.

Forming a bond between a Verndari and an animal is no joke. Most Verndari aren't strong enough to complete such a task. Ori though, she is my fierce badass. I trust her with everything in me, so with one last breath, I leap and land on its back. The heat that I feel is surprisingly soothing. The Phoenix looks back at me. Where I expected anger, I see protectiveness. I soften to the creature, patting its side as a peace treaty. My phoenix seems content after that. She flies off after the others, past the remaining fiery birds and the gapping abyss.

On the other side, a floating island appears. It has a large dome resting on it. The dome itself is at least 3 stories tall. The walls are solid, shimmering in the sunlight. They're opaque enough that shadows are all you can see, hinting at the dome's contents. There are a few trees scatter around the outside of the dome, but not much else. Another archway with purple magic sits right in front of the dome, marking a door that will inevitably take us further on in the trial.

The birds land on the edge of the Island and allow us to dismount. We all patiently wait as Ori puts her hand on the Phoenix's beak and she closes her eyes. The only sign that she is using magic is the glow of her whip at her side.

46: ORI

Don't Underestimate those Around You

-Ljot

I feel my phoenix's desire to stay by my side before I even touch her beak. During the quick trip from the cliff ledge, I have grown attached to her. The minute my hand touches her, she shows me an image of them following us through the archway. My instincts tell me they can't follow us. A tear escapes the phoenix's eyes as I convey this to her. I ensure her that I will see her again by showing her an image of us together.

When my hand finally drops from her beak, all five phoenixes take off and fly to the other side of the dome. I turn toward my men and the archway that awaits us. It stands in front of the dome carrying the same purple magic that brought us here. Another door... just dandy. Walking with as much confidence as I can muster, I walk right past my men and through the purple archway into the next phase of this ridiculous trial, knowing my four guys will follow.

The first steps I take are onto plush green grass. We're looking at a forest of some kind. There is a skinny path with dense trees, thick bushes, and large mushrooms covering the surrounding land. The sky is a green color causing the trees and bushes to blend in, making them hard to see.

I reluctantly walked towards the entrance of the forest, stopping before I step foot on the path. The path awaiting us is made up of wood chips and is only wide enough for two people. Barrett and Orion enter first, pushing all of us into action. Khalid stays by my side as I take my first steps into the forest, leaving Cedrick to bring up the rear. With each step we take deeper into the forest, the cracking of breaking wood sounds underneath our feet announcing our arrival to anyone or anything waiting for us.

The path weaves deeper in the thick brush of the forest, causing what little light we had to diminish down to just a soft glow. When we turn the next corner, I stop in my tracks. Standing in front of me are my two tormentors. I thought I'd never see them again. The grey and white hair on their aged faces stood out amongst the trees. My two tormentors are standing there like they have been expecting me. Their faces look just like they did the last time I saw them... full of hate.

"Because of you, all our kids were taken from us." Foster mother sneered. "I held him back through the years, keeping the torture to a tolerable level, but I see no reason to do that anymore." I scoff at her phrasing, "tolerable level," my ass. There was absolutely nothing tolerable about what they had put me through. Unless she thinks surviving is "tolerable."

As soon as the words left her mouth, my foster father stalks towards me. I keep imagining my guys kicking his ass, but nothing happens. Instead, I am pushed up against a tree. I clamp my eyes shut as I feel his clammy, sweaty hands reach underneath my shirt.

"I have been dreaming of this since your 16th birthday." He says making me want to gag. My eyes snap open in shock at his confession. Yes, I had my suspicions, but my torture never went this far. I look over at my men, needing them to save me. They're just standing there not even looking at me; it's like what he wants to do to me is of no consequence to them. There is no way that is right. My men would never let this happen.

Hope blossoms in my chest as I suspect that this interaction isn't real. They have promised to always protect me; they would die before ever giving up on that promise. I muster up my mental strength to look my tormentor right in the eye. Something I've never had the courage to do.

"You aren't real." I say right before I push him off me. He blinks at me in confusion as I watch him disappear in a shimmer of green magic.

"What the hell." I say out loud, unable to stop myself as I watch my foster mother disappear in the same shimmering green magic as my foster father.

The sound of my voice must have startled it because I suddenly feel little feet walking up my back. Shocked, I turn my head and find a little lizard poking his head at me. He is blue with purple glowing swirls.

"Did you do that?" I ask it. Now I sound crazy. I'm talking to a lizard.

He nods his head at me like he can understand every word I am saying. Being careful not to startle him too much, I slowly reach over to pick him up. Just from the look he gives me, I can tell he is letting me carry him. I suspect that this little guy has a lot of power in him; more power than I want to test at the moment. When I get to the forest's edge, I carefully set him down on the forest floor and watch as he quickly scurries away. His bright purple swirls of magic the only light in the entire forest.

I turn back towards my men. They are all staring into space. I walk around them and see a lizard just like my own locked onto the back of their necks. The lizard's claws are dug deep into their skin and they are biting into their necks. The purple swirls on their scales glowing with the magic it is using. Now how the hell do I get them off?

Khalid:

When we turned the corner of the forest, the Headmaster is waiting for me. What the hell is the

Headmaster doing here in the middle of a trial? "She isn't yours, Khalid. You know that you're not good enough." He tells me vocalizing the fear I have had since I first found out she was my mate.

"I am just as deserving as anyone else." I state, unwilling to give up my woman. Even I hear the uncertainty in my voice. Maybe if I tell myself enough, I will believe it.

"You're not good enough. Why do you think we placed you where we did?" He questions me like I am an Idiot. Upon graduating, they placed me in a position that doesn't allow mates. They kept me as far away from their society as they could manage and even kept my interactions with other Verndari limited. I never found out why they hate me so much, but the position I was given told me everything I needed to know. Through the years, I gave up on the idea of a mate. They took my future away from me, but at the time, I wasn't in a position to change it. Then Ori came along. My knees collapse underneath me at the thought of having to give her up and go back to the life I had before. I was nothing without her.

Cedrick:

A gasp escapes me at what I see. Laying on the ground of the forest are the bodies of all the people I care about. Ryuu, Dain, Gylfi, and my new family, Barrett, Orion, Khalid, but worst of all is Ori. Ori is covered in blood and my heart instantly aches. I feel the pain of a lost bond. My heart aches, my magic tingles under my skin, and my mind rebels against the idea that all the people I love are gone. These people became my family when I had none remaining. Ori became the mate that I always wanted. In the short time we have been together, our bond solidified into a power bond unlike any that has been seen in recent years. I shouldn't be able to live without her. Why am I still alive?

Orion:

Flames quickly became my worst enemy. Walking around the corner and seeing Ori surrounded by fire made me feel helpless; I didn't like feeling helpless. The flames were rising and falling with reds and oranges sparkling in the sky. Sparks were dancing above the flames, flying higher and higher into the dark green sky. Smoke is settled in the circle, obscuring my view of Ori. I couldn't just leave her in there.

I didn't even have time to question how it had happened. All I wanted was to rush past the flames and get her out. My fear was nothing compared to the screams that come from the woman I love. With each scream that pierced the sky, the circle got smaller and smaller.

My feet move of their own accord and I rush towards the flames as they rise high into the sky, closing any gaps I could use to get her out. FUCK!

Barrett:

"You never wanted a mate" my father says as I turn the corner of the forest. How the hell did he get here? I think, as I glare at the man I've not seen in 23 years. Standing tall and proud in the center of the forest path, he looks at me with his left eyebrow raised. His black hair is wavy and sits on his shoulders. Wearing his signature robes, he looks out of place in the forest. But he hasn't changed one bit. There was a reason I left after all.

"I didn't understand what having a mate meant back then. I do now." I say defending my past self.

"Does she know?" my dad asked, cockiness leaking into his tone.

"I never told her. I love her. That is all that matters." I answer, hoping I sound more confident than I am. Truthfully, I am terrified that she will hate me if she ever found out that I didn't want a mate. The only person I had to model a relationship on was my father. My father and mother had a toxic relationship; one that I had no desire to replicate. While my father was not physically abusive, my mother would cave to his wishes. I'd listen to him talk down to her every day. I feared that I would turn into the man I hated. That was before. Now I'm confident I could never be like him.

I look over at my shoulder at Ori, praying that she won't hate me. Only darkness stands in the spot where she once stood. Where the hell is she? "ORI!!!" I scream, trying to find her.

My father, seemingly oblivious to my panic, continues to sow seeds of doubt into my mind. "I wonder if her feelings for you would change if she found out? Would she still love you?"

"YES, SHE WOULD STILL LOVE ME." I Scream at him, unable to ignore his jabs. "WHERE THE FUCK IS SHE?"

Ori:

Khalid dropping to his knees solidified my decision on which lizard to remove first. Going on instinct alone, I stroke the lizard from its head to its tail. At first you can see the lizard tense, but soon it relaxes at my touch, enjoying the feel of being petted. When I see its teeth release from Khalid's neck, I pull it off him. Almost instantly you see Khalid coming back to his senses.

"It was this little guy I explain." Holding the lizard up to him before releasing him and watching him scurry off in the same direction as his friend.

"That's an Ottazard. Fuck they brought out the big guns for this one didn't they."

"We all knew they would. Come on. Let's get them off the others."

"How?" He asks, looking at the lizard that's clamped on the back of Cedrick's neck. "We're taught that only the individual in the hallucination can get the Ottazard to release."

"Well, that just isn't true. I got yours off you, I can certainly help the other men as well." I insist.

Khalid watches as I carefully pet the Ottazard until it releases Barrett. He raises his eyes in shock that no magic was involved. At least there was one benefit to living with the humans, I think, as I work down the line of my men, releasing them one by one.

When all four of my men are finally free from their fears, I'm quickly squeezed in a massive hug. They needed to feel me and know I was safe. I needed it too. I am glad I'm surrounded by all four of my men. In those seconds, I feel safe again. I sigh when they all press light kisses to my cheek, knowing our hug was going to end.

"I am so glad you are okay." Orion says.

"I thought I had lost you." Cedrick says with tears in his eyes.

"Come on. Let's get this shit over with." I say, trying to focus on the task at hand.

"How did you get the Ottazards off? They're not known for releasing their victims." Orion asks as we continue our way down the trail. Unfortunately for him, he was the last one released from the Ottazard's hold so he didn't get to experience the wonders of my human side.

"I just coaxed them off."

"You coaxed them off." He repeats stunned while the other guys are laughing their asses off. This right here. This is what I love.

47: RYUU

During Times in Life when Allies are Rare, Protect those Relationships.

-Ljot

Dain and I positioned ourselves in the stands specifically so that we could keep our eyes on everything. A purple orb was overhead, allowing us to view the entire trial as Ori progresses through it. Honestly, I've been mighty impressed with her. Her actions have been unconventional, but effective.

"Have you been watching the councilmen?" Dain ask from next to me.

"Yes." I respond, letting my eyes go to the Council for the hundredth time. They're sitting opposite of us on the main floor, front and center, just like we knew they would. They always like taking credit for their "artwork" regardless of the outcome.

All the councilmen and women are present; they're required to be here. From here, all I can do is watch their expressions, and hope they give something away that will help narrow down our pool of suspects. The councilman that is sitting there picking his fingernails is the least of my problems. He is evidently uninterested in the trial. At least I can cross one person off the list.

It's those of the Council that have an unusually high interest in the trial that I am most concerned about; there are three in total. The Headmaster being one of them. Out of the three, the Headmaster is the least of my concerns. He has protected and saved Ori since she arrived on Campus. Plus, when Ori made it past all those Phoenixes, his shoulders relaxed in relief. It's obvious he cares about her.

The other two are a different story. If you watch them close enough, you could see their jaws tensing when she made it past an obstacle. They both want her to fail.

The first is a councilwoman that has a well-known hatred for strong, confident woman. So, it's no surprise that she isn't a fan of Ori. The Councilwoman helped start the traditions we have in place that creates nothing but needy, weak woman who are dependent on their men. She likes it like that. Woman like Lulu and Ori are a problem to her. She designed Lulu's trial and almost got her killed. Lulu was in the infirmary for a month before she was healthy enough to leave with her men. All of them have held a grudge against the Council ever since. Which is why the Headmaster was surprised they came back so quickly.

The other person is the oldest Councilmen we have. He has always been a power hunger individual. The white of his hair is an outward sign to others of how much power he has. People have always suspected that his power is the only reason he survived the death of his mates. It has been 18 years since the last of them died and he is still as strong as he was prior to their deaths, which in our world is unheard of. Losing your mate is supposed to weaken you. It's part of the reason why mates are cherished; we can never grow into our full potential without them.

While most in the community pitied him for losing his mate, I suspected his lack of magical change meant more than him just being powerful. I have other theories. I suspect he killed his mates by stealing their magic. It would explain how he could remain so powerful without their presence, but I could never find proof. If I did, he'd be locked up by now.

Since his mate died, no one has come along that was as powerful as him. Ori is the first, and he definitely sees her as a threat. He is powerful in his focus magic, but she has the power of all four. Something that he has craved for years. My sources tell me he has hunted for the power of all four. His agitation and aggression grows stronger with each year he fails to gain the power he craves. A man like him doesn't need power.

"Holy Shit" Dain says next to me, shock suddenly lacing his voice.

I look up at the trial and find that the Ottazards have latched onto all five of them. It isn't easy to escape an Ottazard. Even those individuals with experience have died at their claws. They may be small, but they are powerful little creatures that make you hallucinate your worst fears. The images are so real you can't tell that you are hallucinating. You can feel, see, and hear everything like it was actually happening.

The arena at this point is on pins and needles waiting for them all to drop. Looking around, you can see people shaking their heads. Tears coming out of some eyes. They are all assuming she is going to die here. I really hope they are wrong.

I am relieved when Ori finally comes out of it. You hear her say, "that wasn't very nice" to the Ottazard that is now in her hand like he was her pet. The gasp that escapes everyone isn't surprising. Ottazards don't let you touch them. But one by one she removes the creatures from her men, using no magic at all. Very human of her; I smile because I'm liking her more and more. I guarantee our killer didn't think of her human tendencies as a strength. Will they help her survive this ordeal? I hope so. She is stronger than any of them gave her credit for.

48: ORI

Magical Creatures are a Wonderful Part of Our Society

-Ljot

Walking through the forest should be a relaxing experience. For me, walking amongst nature was always peaceful, but this is different. Instead of relaxed, I'm tense, and it seems to get worse with every breaking stick, chirping insect, and howling animal; the hairs on my arms stand on end in anticipation for what is coming next. After real life phoenixes and lizards that make you live your worst fears, what is going to be next?

Unknown:

I'm sitting with the rest of the Council watching the trial. I underestimated her. I expected her to die right away; with her lack of experience in magic, she shouldn't have been able to get as far as she has. Watching her in action though, she's different from the others; I should have anticipated that. Planning her trial as if she as was a normal Verndari female was a mistake on my part. She isn't a normal Verndari and she never will be. Forgetting that fact was stupid on my part.

As Ori passed each phase, my magic becomes more volatile. I can feel it under my skin, itching to get out and finish her itself. Ori's a threat. It doesn't like that she has the potential to be more powerful. It wants to do what it has always done when it has felt threatened... eliminate the threat.

Now is not the time. I have to be patient. Unfortunately, my magic is not very patient; it's taking most of my energy to keep it contained. The minute I slip, people will know of our involvement. I can never let that happen.

Ori:

After an hour of wandering the woods, we come to an abrupt stop as we make it to another cliff edge. Looking out across the sky you can see the faint outline of another arch and the purple glow of magic signaling the existence of another doorway.

At first glance, all you saw was an empty void between here and the next archway. But a shimmering on the right draws my attention. It takes a minute, but eventually I see the faint outline of what reminds me of the ropes course Ryuu and Lulu ran me through. This one though is a ropes course on crack. Why? because it's invisible. You heard me right; it's invisible. They couldn't make this easy, could they?

"How the hell are we supposed to get over there?" Orion asks, befuddled.

"We have to navigate the ropes course." I say while I silently thank Ryuu and Lulu for all the crazy training they have put me through. I was cursing them at the time, but now I am immensely grateful for every pain and sore muscle I got because of their craziness. I'd be lost right now if not for them.

"What course?" Barrett asks, oblivious to what sits in front of us. "All I see is open sky."

"The invisible one." I say, as I slide to the right until I am in front of the first rope that dangles down from the sky. I lean forward just enough to grab a hold of the rope, gripping it easily. After tugging slightly to ensure the rope is stable, I leap onto the rope and start my ascent, unsure of exactly how high up I'll be going.

Below me I hear Khalid say, "fuck" as I feel a small tug on the rope. I glance down and the shock on his face tells me that just like Barrett, he can't see a damn thing. This is going to be interesting. "Come on." I urge.

When I finally reach a platform, the first thing I notice is how small it is; at approximately two feet by two feet, there is barely enough room for two people. I suspect every platform along the way will all be that way. Which means I'll have to be constantly on the move to ensure no one gets stuck on any obstacle.

Looking down, it appears I am standing on thin air; the only reassuring sight being the faint outline of the platform I am standing on. If I couldn't see the shimmering outline, I'd be freaking out. No wonder the guys are swearing behind me.

When Khalid arrives at my side, I take it as my signal to move. The next rope is horizontal with the ground making it tempting to look down. Don't look down, I repeat to myself over and over as I grab a hold of the rope and allow myself to dangle. Swinging my legs up so they're crossed over the top of the rope, I slowly start scooting down the rope one inch at a time.

I'm about halfway down when I hear Khalid behind me, cursing again. "I CAN'T FIND IT ORI!" He screams at me in a panic. I lean my head back to get a look at him and Cedrick who is at his side. Both Barrett and Orion are stuck on the rope below the platform. Orion's shaky arms are visible; they are going to give out soon.

I stop in my tracks and allow my magic to guide me. It flows through me to the rope I'm holding. Soon, the rope is pulsing with my magic, allowing my men to easily see its location and follow. Neat, I think as the rope lights up a beautiful red. I didn't know I could do that. I smile at myself before I continue along the rope until I reach a dead end.

The platform I expected to find at the end doesn't exist. Instead, about three feet away you see

the perpendicular outline of my next stop. I let go of
the rope with my hands, allowing my feet to hold me.
I take a moment to glance back and make sure all four
guys are on the rope. Once the last of my mates
makes it on to the rope, I swing my body trying to get
myself as close as I can before letting go with my legs.
I allow my momentum to carry me forward and grasp
onto... a bar? What the HELL?

"FUCK" I hear from all my men behind me. I
chuckle, suspecting the rope disappeared on them. I
wish I could see their faces; that would be a sight to
see.

"Crazy ass motherfuckers." Khalid continues,
letting a slew of swear words escape his lips.

"Don't worry. I've got you guys." I say as I
close my eyes and form two balls of energy, one on
either end of the bar I am holding. I take a minute to
shoot a ball of magic on either end of the bar. Once
they are settled on the ends, I start a flow of magic
from one ball to the other. I forced the magic into a
momentum that becomes natural, allowing my magic
to continue on its own accord. Once satisfied, I swing
and leap over to the waiting platform a couple feet
away on the other side of the bar. I look over and
Khalid was mid leap off the rope to the bar. My other
three men have terrified looks on their faces and
continue their trek down the rope that they can no
longer see.

The way across the sky is slow, but steady. I
take a moment on each obstacle to make sure it is lit
up, ensuring my men will make it across safely. When

I finally reach the archway, I am relieved. My arms and legs are burning, and I can feel the toll my use of magic had on my body. I'm weak, but there is no way I'm saying that out loud. Honestly, I don't know how much more of that I would have been able to handle.

I turn around and see the sky lit up with the brilliant red of my magic. It's beautiful. If they weren't intent on trying to kill me, I would have actually enjoyed this challenge. But let's keep that a secret between us.

I anxiously watch all four of my mates. One slip and they would fall to their death. My heart wouldn't be able to handle losing one of them. It feels like my heart is high in my chest trying to escape. It isn't until the last of them arrives at my side that my heart finally settles back into my chest.

"Let's not do that again." Barrett says when he arrives at my side.

"That wasn't fun for you, Barrett?" I ask, trying to tease him.

"No." He says huffing. "I hate heights. That..." he starts as he points to the sky "was terrifying."

"You can fly through the one on campus." Orion begins.

"I can fucking see that one." He answers in a scream. "Who makes a fucking invisible ropes course? Who even thinks of that shit?"

"The Council." The rest of us answer simultaneously. Even I know they are in charge of coming up with this shit.

"Barrett," I say soothingly. "When we get out of here, I can promise you'll never have to do that again. But I don't know what is that way." I point to the archway that is sitting there waiting for us.

"Fine. Let's get this shit over with." Barrett says as he leads the way through the next archway.

49: BARRETT

Expect the unexpected

-Ljot

Most trials only have three parts to them, so I'm praying that the archway in front of me leads us back to the stadium. I knew immediately that we weren't that lucky. If the lack of stone walls wasn't an indication, the magic that pierced my shoulder like an arrow was definitely a clue. I couldn't stop my scream as the magic burned my skin during its travel through my shoulder. Very little blood was spilled, for which I am grateful, but you can smell my burnt flesh.

I hear Ori's gasp from next to me as she dodges a stream of magic and falls to the ground next to me. Before I even realize what Ori is doing, I'm being dragged behind a large boulder. I wince in pain but open my eyes as soon as I feel my back resting on the rock. "Fuck that hurt." I mutter to no one in particular.

Ori:

I fall to the ground as soon as I step through the archway. Magic barely misses me as it flies over my head. I look down at Barrett and notice the hole in his shoulder. Seconds later, the smell of burnt flesh hits my nose and my stomach immediately starts churning; I try to block out my sense of smell as I drag him behind a large boulder that is sitting to the side. "Fuck that hurt." He grumbles as his back touches the rock.

With magic flying over our heads, I carefully peek around the corner of our hiding spot. "What the fuck!" I exclaim, having no other words to describe what I am seeing.

About three hundred feet away, another archway sits. If my suspicions are correct, it's going to be the way out. The creature guarding the archway stands at ten feet tall with black skin and horns that curl upward. Skimming across his skin is an orange tone that makes his skin look like flowing lava. In his hands he holds two magical spheres. As if he can sense me watching him, he shoots magic at my head. I dart back behind the boulder and hear his magic hit the rock, creating chipped off shards that scatter all around.

I crouch in front of Barrett and tell him to stay there. Before he can protest, I stand up facing the creature that is blocking our way to freedom. The next time he sends magic at me, I redirect it back to him. I watch as his magic gets absorbed back into his skin.

The absorbed magic creates a flowing wave on his skin. He smirks at me like I just did him a favor.

I take out my whip and let my magic flow as I analyze the monster in front of me. As my guys gather at my back, Barrett included, I feel their magic joining mine; my whip, now carrying magic from all five of us, glows bright red at my side. I can feel the power that flows through it, begging to be released.

My mind is battling itself right now. All I want is to yell at Barrett and tell him to sit down and let the rest of us handle it. The other half of my mind knows I need his magic to get past whatever this creature is.

Putting my fear for Barrett aside, I let my whip fly and watch as it wraps around the creature's wrist. I pull, trying to create a tighter grip, but with a flick of the creature's wrist, my whip flies out of my hand and onto the ground five feet in front of me. The creature roars in obvious anger and shoots more magic right at us. My whip moves on its own accord, meeting the creature's magic midair. Upon contact, his magic dissipates; I watch him as he flinches in pain at the destruction of his magic.

Suddenly, I understand the flowing quality of his skin. He's made of magic. To destroy his magic is to destroy him. Interesting. My whip finishes its flight towards me and lands at my feet. With the creature in pain, I have just enough time to grab my whip and let it fly wrapping around his ankles. I pull hard on my whip, using Khalid's magic to tighten and strengthen my hold. His ankles clash together increasing his anger causing a roar to escape him. As he throws his magic around wildly, the five of us duck and dodge his magic as it flies over our heads. One ball of magic narrowly missing me by inches.

I feel Cedrick's hands suddenly clasping over mine as Barrett and Orion dive in opposite directions, dodging yet another ball of magic. We both pull on the whip as hard as we can, finally causing the creature to fall to the ground with a thud.

Within my whip, Orion's magic flows and confirms my suspicions; the creature is made of pure magic. As if a switch has been hit, Cedrick's magic impatiently starts pulling the creature's magic from its essence. With each particle that's removed, the Monster in front of us shrinks. You can see its dark magic traveling up my whip. We are playing a game of tug-of-war with his dark magic, both fighting for control. About halfway up my whip, smoke radiates where Barrett's magic destroys every particle of the Monster's magic it encounters.

It is a slow process, but you can see him weakening. He is withering in the whip's hold. As we destroy more of his magic, the less of a struggle he is making and the easier it is to pull his magic from him. When bags form under his eyes and smoke radiates from his limbs, I sense we are close to ending him. When the last of his magic is drained from him, he disappears in a cloud of black smoke.

Seconds later, I hear a thud behind me which causes me to whip around. Barrett collapsed onto the ground. Between the wound on his shoulder that still hasn't healed, and my excessive use of his magic; he's drained. Orion quickly scoops him up into his arms. I smile at my men, thinking the trial is finally over.

"How the hell did you survive?" A deep angry voice says from behind me.

50: UNKNOWN

The Enemy is closer than you realize

-Ljot

My fury mounts the further into the trial Ori gets. She skillfully maneuvers through the rope course as if she can see it. That should be impossible.

Ori and her men should have gotten stuck on the cliff or plummeted to their deaths when their trial first started. I would have been happy with either option.

So, when all five of them make it to the other side of the ropes course, I am thankful I put my insurance policy at the end of the trial. I didn't tell the others on the Council about him. They would have over-ruled me. Better to ask forgiveness than permission.

The creature guarding the end gate is one of legends. Everyone knows of their existence, but very few have seen them. I have been training him for this moment for centuries. He knows that his freedom is at stake; he won't let me down.

"Where the hell did you get him?" the councilman next to me asks in an agitated whisper.

"I have a few connections." I state not wanting them to know that I created him. I bring my focus back to the trial and smile when my creature wastes no time piercing Barrett's shoulder. The fools went through the portal unprepared for what was on the other side. I'm sure the smile that crosses my face is huge; I knew my creature wouldn't let me down.

Ryuu:

The reality of what we are facing was obvious as soon as I saw him smile. It had to be him. I kept my eyes on the councilman as Dain watched the trial. I knew it wasn't going well. Not only because the councilman's smile got wider, but also because Dain's swearing got a lot more colorful.

That is until I hear a "Hell Yeah!" from next to me. The man I'm watching stands up and slams his fists on the table in front of him. He stays standing and stupidly allows his fury to become more evident as the creature deteriorates.

When the stadium screams in triumph, the man in question storms forward and creates a portal walking right through it. Within seconds we see him standing with Ori and her men. "How the hell did you survive?" He asks, not caring that he just incriminated himself.

"We have to get over there." I tell Dain.

"We don't know where there is." Dain says, stating the obvious.

"Don't worry. I'm about to find out." I tell Dain as I stalk over to where the remaining Council members are sitting.

They all watch me as I cross the main floor and make a beeline for them. The Headmaster isn't surprised to see me; the rest of them though are a different story.

"What are you doing here, Ryuu?" the councilwoman asks. "You know you can't be here."

"Where are they?" I demand.

"You know we can't tell you. It is against the rules for anyone to interfere." She responds.

"That rule is now null and void, as one of your own is interfering right now." I say pointing up to the magical screen just as he shoots magic at the five of them.

"That may be true, but we still won't tell you." She says letting everyone here know that she would be all too happy if Ori died in her trial. Bitch.

Ori:

The man glaring at me has the same silver hair that makes up half my hair. His menacing eyes are the same charcoal grey color that stares back at me through the mirror every morning. Holy Shit is this who I think it is?

Unknown/Silas-Thorne:

Seeing the young woman for the first time up close is a shock to my system. I thought she was dead. I was furious that morning when I found out her mother went to the hospital without me. I knew my mate was up to something, but I couldn't prove it. My mate was a very smart woman; she knew I was going to drain our child of her powers. I thought I had broken her of her rebellious ways when I killed her other mates and raped her. I watch her fear of me intensify as I drained her mates of their magic and then strangled them right in front of her. I got off on the fear and enjoyed every minute of the rape. The best part... I positioned her so she had to look at the dead bodies of her other mates the entire time I fucked her. It was glorious.

She apparently wasn't as broken as I thought. When I arrived at the hospital, I was told our daughter was a stillbirth. The devastation I felt from her as well as the tears streaming down her face made me believe her. I even let her live for a while after that, hoping we'd have another girl I could drain. When she failed to get pregnant, I killed her. She no longer had a purpose to me. I guess I underestimated her.

It doesn't surprise me that the woman who has caused all this grief was my own daughter. Who else could father one so powerful? Yeah… I'm a cocky bastard. The silver in her hair is just like mine, and her charcoal eyes are like looking in a mirror. The red though… she got that from her mother. I can't believe I didn't see it sooner.

I see her men looking between Ori and me; one by one you see it clicking as they realize who she is. All Verndari know of the death of my baby girl. Our community mourned the devastating loss of yet another Verndari female for years. Our community has learned how precious each female is as we went from 4500 to the 103 females. We've been hunted to the point that our extinction is on the horizon.

My beliefs though… everyone else could die for all I care. I'd drain all 103 women of their powers if I thought I could get away with it. Power is all that matters to me. I can't allow anyone, my daughter included, to live if they threaten the power I hold.

With her mate's standing in shock, I use the distraction to my advantage. I throw my magic right at them. Unfortunately for me, my daughter is stronger than I give her credit for; she throws a shield up in front of them faster than anyone so young should be able to. She has been training for mere days. What she just did shouldn't be possible.

"You're the one trying to kill me?" Ori asks. "My own fucking father is trying to kill me. What the Hell!" She screams. I am surprised she figured it out so fast.

"I didn't know you were my baby girl till now, but that doesn't change a thing. I still would've tried to kill you. Can't have someone stronger than me. The power you have should be mine. If I had gotten to you as a baby like I planned, I'd have all the power that runs through your veins. Unfortunately, your mother was smarter than I ever gave her credit for and she hid you from me. I didn't even think to look for you with the humans. Too bad I can't kill her again." I sneer, meaning every word. I would give her mother a painful death if she was still around.

51: ORI

Family is More than Blood.

-Ljot

As my father is talking, I sense their presence. My phoenix has her flames down to just a small ember, allowing her to stealthily come up behind the man that is trying to kill me. I know little about him, but it is easy to tell that he is powerful and power hungry. His focus is solely on his mission to kill me. Did he forget we are still in my trial? Does he realize he confessed to murder and attempted murder in front of most of the Verndari people? Everyone back at the school would have heard his confession. *Does his confession surprise them?* I ponder as he tells me how being his daughter changes nothing. I'm not his daughter. In order to be his daughter, he has to actually give a damn about me. He can go rot in hell for all I care.

My "father" rants like he has been planning this speech for years. I just let him drone on, happy for the delay. It gives me some much-needed time to think, not that it helps much. As soon as his diatribe is over, he lets another ball of magic loose towards us, causing my shield to shutter as it gets hit. I can feel my shield weakening with every hit of his magic. My shield isn't going to last much longer.

Behind him, my phoenix squawks right before she shoots fire at the man. My jaw drops as he goes up in flames. You can see him starting to extinguish the flames. I can't allow that to happen. Now is my chance. I let my shield drop and take advantage of that moment. I shoot magical ropes out at him, tying both his hands and feet up. Cedrick and Khalid rush him and grab a hold of him just as the last flame dies. He's now scarred from the Phoenix fire. I should probably feel bad about that, but I'm not. Instead, I walk over to my phoenix and put my hand on the side of her head. "Thanks for protecting me." I tell her with gratitude.

The other four phoenixes land at her side. Within seconds I hear, "What the hell are they doing here?" from Orion.

"They go where we go. They're a little protective of us now." Orion just looks at me like I am insane if I think we are keeping them. "She really is sorry." I tell Orion which just makes his jaw drop.

"How do you know she is sorry?" He asks genuinely curious.

"She told me." I say as I watch the Phoenix that burnt Orion slowly walk up to him. The phoenix is a very smart creature. He walks slowly, trying not to startle Orion. I don't blame him; Orion is a little jumpy. We all watch in awe as the Phoenixes fire changes to a beautiful white flame.

"What is she doing?" Orion says with panic in his voice. Orion's phoenix gets about a foot from him before stopping; he can sense that Orion won't let him get any closer right now.

"She is trying to apologize." I say. "Now turn around." When I get no response from Orion, I add a trust me to the request. We hear a loud sigh before he finally does as I ask. The only reason he is doing it is because I asked him; he wouldn't have turned around for anyone else. Seconds later, we watch as the white flame caresses over his burnt skin. When the flame finally disappears, his skin is good as new, but with a small black phoenix now tattooed where the damage was. It is a blessing from his Phoenix.

"Make him heal me!" My father demands, having seen with his own eyes what a phoenix is truly capable of. He's in no position to make any demands, but the power-hungry man doesn't seem to understand that.

"I can't make him heal you even if I wanted to. They have to decide on their own that they want to heal you, or it won't work. Surely you know that?" I say, unable to keep the frustration from my tone.

"They don't allow criminals to be healed anyway, Silas-Thorne." Khalid says as he tightens his hold on the man. "You know that considering you're the one that created that particular rule." Khalid finishes adding salt to his wounds.

"I'm not a criminal." He says trying to defend himself.

"I'm sure the stadium of people that heard you confess to killing my mother would disagree with you." I state as I make my way to the final doorway. Before I enter, I look over my shoulder... Cedrick and Khalid are dragging Silas-Thorne, aka my father, Orion is helping to support a still wobbly Barrett, and all five phoenixes are bringing up the rear.

Ryuu:

I pace in front of the Council as we watch and wait. Either Silas-Thorne is going to kill them all or we are going to have a councilman to arrest. The next few minutes are the most shocking of my life. What we witness will go down in history. Not only did a Phoenix defend a Verndari, which is unheard of, they also healed one. Rumors of their healing flame have been passed down through the generations, but I don't know a single soul who has ever seen it in real life. "Holy Fucking Shit!" Dain screams from next to me. "Tell me you fucking saw that?!" He screams excitedly like I just gave him a Christmas present.

"Yes, I saw that!" I began chuckling, enjoying his rare enthusiasm.

When they finally walked through the gate, Phoenixes in tow, I made sure there were people I trusted ready to arrest Silas-Thorne. I wasn't going to allow his power to get him out of this one.

52: ORI

Love Life and all the Joys it brings you

-Ljot

O ur phoenixes stayed close to us the entire time we were in the colosseum. I could sense that they were on guard. My phoenix was afraid Silas-Thorne would escape; none of the phoenixes relaxed until Silas-Thorne was dragged out of the colosseum and completely out of their sight.

By that time, the entire Council had risen to their feet. They stood waiting with straight faces. Reaching out with my magic, I tried to get a read on them but failed miserably; my magic was still too weak from everything I just went through. Guess I get to find out my fate the good old-fashioned way... waiting until they were ready to tell me.

The seconds ticked by feeling like an eternity, but eventually we're ushered forward so we would be standing in front of them. Our phoenixes were suspended in flight behind us, ready to defend us if needed. They don't trust the Council. I am glad we have the protective creatures on our side, but I hope they don't have to defend us again. While I agree with their untrusting assessment of the Council, I hope in time the Council will earn my trust. Only time will tell.

I know little about the logistics of the trial, but I pray that I get to go live life with my men by my side. I was told that was the reward for making it through their trial. After everything that has happened to me, I am skeptical that it'll actually happen; part of me is assuming they have a Plan B. Most cruel people in the world do.

As we stand there waiting, the colosseum is so quiet you could hear a pin drop. I suspect that everyone here is just as curious about my fate as I am. It wouldn't surprise me if most Verndari present assumed I'd die in the trial, never to reach the end where my fate is decided.

"To be honest with you, Ori, I am surprised you survived. Your techniques were unique, but effective." The councilwoman states confirming my suspicions. *They shouldn't have put me in the trial to begin with.* I think as I bite my tongue to stop myself from issuing any kind of retort. I am assuming snapping at her wouldn't work in my favor.

"I, for one, knew you could do it." The Headmaster says. His sincerity contrasts with the others on the Council and is very refreshing. I am glad we have at least one person on the Council we can trust.

"Thank you, Headmaster." I say politely, as I smile right at him. I want him to know how much his faith means to me.

"Usually when you pass your trial, it means that you get placed for work, but your circumstances are different. You have not been at school long enough to learn how to use magic properly, so you'll stay for the time being." The Councilwoman says smirking at me. She obviously thinks she won this one.

"I would like to disagree with you on that one." The Headmaster says speaking up. I knew he was on our side. "Throughout the entire trial, she had control of her magic. Besides that, we're required to see if any teams want to take them on; it's written in the laws. Section 367, part 3 states that any student that passes their trial can join any team that petitions to take them on. They're only required to stay and repeat the trial when the student or mating group is not accepted by a team, section 368 part 2."

"No one will want someone who knows about a week of magic." She states like her feelings are enough.

"You don't know that." I protest, unwilling to let her take my future away from me. "We won't be accepted by anyone if the question isn't even raised. If you didn't want someone to take us on, you shouldn't have put me in the trial in the first place. As it stands, you did place me in the trial, and I passed. I have the same rights as anyone else who passed. I will freely stay and repeat the trial if no team wants to take me and my mates on." I say, looking her straight in the eye.

"We will take them." Ryuu states firmly. "We have enough space that she can learn more magic undetected. We will even help train her." He finishes giving another reason on how my departure from the school won't do any harm.

"You don't need any more people." She argues back.

"Since when is having a few extra hands a bad thing. It'll give us a wider array of skills to use and allow my men the luxury of vacations. Breaks that we currently aren't given, but desperately need from time to time."

"You cannot deny his request." The Headmaster states firmly. "There's no limit to the amount of team members he can have. Besides, he can request them, especially since one of Ori's mate's is already part of his team. It is the most logical choice."

"Fine." She says eventually conceding. "Congrats on graduating Ori. You and your mates are now part of Ryuu's team. Get the hell out of here before I change my mind." She grumbles.

Even a blind man could tell how unhappy she is with the decision, but I'll take it. She doesn't have to tell me twice. The five of us, followed by our phoenixes, Ryuu, and Dain, leave that Colosseum before anyone could process what she said. Seriously, get me out of this place. I'll be happy if I never see it again.

EPILOGUE: THE MISTRESS

Don't Let Anyone take your Happily Ever After

-Ljot

M y heels click-clack on the cement floor of the prison. The cell at the far end of the hall holds Silas-Thorne. The white of his hair stands out against the dark grey cement interior. The only light comes from the magic buzzing between bars, keeping all types of magical creatures contained. As I walk down the corridor, I pass other Verndari as well as Vampires, Werewolves, and Dragons just to name a few. Some individuals are here because of the hideous acts they have committed, while others are here because of the threat they pose. Too bad I couldn't just lock Ori up and throw away the key.

It's been two weeks since Silas-Thorne snapped and exposed his involvement in the attempted killings of Ori. There's nothing I could do to keep him out of prison; too many of our kind were present for his outburst.

While I wanted to come sooner, I couldn't without looking suspicious. So far, no one knows of my involvement, and I plan on keeping it that way.

"What the Hell were you thinking?" I chastise him as I approach his cell.

"My anger got the best of me." He admits turning around to look me in the eyes.

"No shit." I tell him as I walk as close to his cell as feasible. "You aren't any good to me in here. You were my best shot of removing her." I tell him as I get my first good look at him since the trial. Most of his exposed skin is covered with scars from the phoenix fire. Those are scars that'll never heal, a constant reminder of his failure.

"Let me out then." He says like I can just wave my hands and release him.

"You are aware I have no control of our prisons. Sit tight but be ready."

"Ready for what?" He asks me as I turn and leave him to his cell. He needs time in here to ponder his stupidity. Silas-Thorne getting locked up put my plans even further behind. That's okay, I'll just have to improvise.

ORI:

It wasn't until we made it back to Ryuu's place that he broke the news of Gylfi. Cedrick felt a mixture of shock, betrayal, and grief at the loss. I felt every emotion of his pain. Gylfi was like a brother to him, so Cedrick took his death hard, but not as hard as the betrayal. Mates are sacred to all Verndari, or so he thought. His brother trying to kill me, his mate, was like a stab to his heart. I was there for him, along with Barrett, Orion, and Khalid, anytime he needed us. Supporting him through his pain brought all five of us even closer together as mates.

We've been at Ryuu's house for the last two weeks. It may not technically be my home, but I quickly fell in love with the place. He explained how important it was for the team to live together. Not only did it help the team bond; it also made it easier to leave on a moment's notice. Which he said was an unfortunate aspect of the job.

At first, I wondered if having Ryuu and Dain with us would bother me, but it doesn't. If anything, it made me feel like I had a bigger family. Not having a proper family before, I loved having everyone together. Ryuu and Dain easily let Barrett and Orion into their group. The six men in the house have quickly built genuine camaraderie. The guys tease each other daily and I love watching the back-and-forth banter. You could feel the love in the house, and I wouldn't have it any other way.

Ryuu ended up giving me free rein on two of the bedrooms. I hated not having all my men with me each night, so we ended up modifying the two rooms, so they are one gigantic room. We also had to get a customized bed so that all five of us could sleep together. The guys will occasionally fight over who gets to sleep next to me like right now.

"You slept next to her yesterday." Cedrick argued with Khalid. He has made the same point four times already, but Khalid isn't relenting. Standing in the door to our bathroom in nothing but a robe, I watch on allowing them to continue their arguing for a few more minutes. Fights like these always make me feel loved. Deciding there has been enough, I intentionally walk up to my guys and drop my robe. The arguing immediately stops and I am quickly lifted up by Barrett and laid down on our bed.

"That is one way to stop a fight" Barrett smirks as he begins kissing me. A second set of lips descends on my thighs, causing me to shiver in anticipation. "I think you're ready." He declares after releasing my lips. My eyes dilate with desire, knowing exactly what they have planned.

"Get on all fours." Cedrick commands from the foot of the bed. Barrett lets me go and I eagerly flip over and get into position. "Spread your legs open further." Each command he gives me makes me wetter for my men. The dip of the bed behind me indicating that one of my men has gotten on the bed. Hands grab a hold of my hips and caress my body until they reach my shoulder. In one smooth motion, he grabs ahold of my hair and forces my head up. I watch as Barrett climbs on the bed and slides underneath me. My hands go to his shoulders as he grips my hips. "Ride me, sweetheart." He whispers in my ear as he pulls my hips down, allowing me to spear myself on his dick. I moan at the feel of him inside me.

Orion and Khalid are now kneeling in front of me. I watch them stroke themselves as they watch. Behind me, I feel the tip of Cedrick's dick press against my anus. I whimper at the strange feeling. By the time he's fully seated inside of me, I'm close to the edge. It's the first time I've ever felt two of my men inside of me at once. It is wonderfully full feeling. It's even better when they start moving in tandem.

I'm so lost in the feelings I can no longer look at the two men waiting their turn. The first time I fly over the edge, I bring Barrett with me. Cedrick stops just long enough for Barrett to slip out of me and for Khalid to enter. I moan when they start moving again. With each stroke, my moans get louder and louder. When Cedrick finally explodes deep inside of me, he gently pulls out, allowing Orion to take his place. Five orgasms later, the five of us are all satisfied and spent collapsed on the bed.

I was just drifting off to sleep when there was a knock at the door.

"Yes." Cedrick groans from next to me.

"Can you bring Ori out here?" Ryuu asks from the other side of the door.

"I'll be right there." I answer, knowing Ryuu wouldn't ask if it wasn't important. Five minutes later, I'm walking to the living room with my guys close behind me. I stop dead in my tracks when I see a young girl sitting on the couch with her knees pulled up to her chest. Her hair is cut short, with one side buzzed, while the other side goes down to her chin.

"Hello…" I begin as I slowly approach her, not wanting to startle her. "what's your name?" I ask as I kneel in front of her.

"Senza."

"That's a beautiful name."

"Don't call the Council." She asks pleading with me to listen.

"You're a Verndari." I say more to myself than her. "When do you turn 18?" I ask suspecting it's soon.

"In an hour." She admits. "I don't want to be forced into these horrid traditions. Please, just let me stay here. I won't be a bother."

"I know you won't." I tell her as I look up at my men who are already speaking with Dain and Ryuu. How can she go through her awakening without the Council being made aware? How long do we have to find her mates? What the Hell are we going to do?

COMING SOON...

SENZA: THE REBEL
VERNDARI

ABOUT THE AUTHOR

Hi. I'm Oriana Star. I love to read and at the encouragement of others, I started writing and quickly fell in love with the art. I love writing fiction as there are no boundaries to what my imagination can create.

My current obsession is Fantasy Romance and I hope you enjoy the characters and the world I have created.

Oriana lives in Michigan with her Husband and Two daughters. In my spare time I enjoy swimming and pushing myself past my fears to create a better me.

www.ingramcontent.com/pod-product-compliance
Lightning Source LLC
Chambersburg PA
CBHW071451170626
46811CB00007B/2541